Pumpkin Squash

ᴬ Tiger Lily's Café® Mystery

By Kathleen Thompson

Kathleen Thompson

Pumpkin Squash

Volume 8

ᴬ Tiger Lily's Café® Mystery

By Kathleen Thompson

Poems fully or partially recited in Chapter 13: *Jabberwocky*, by Lewis Carroll, and *The Road Not Taken*, by Robert Frost.

ISBN-13: 978-0-9984023-7-6

ISBN-10: 0-9984023-7-0

© Registration # TX 8-429-796

Library of Congress Control Number: 2017906684

Kathleen Thompson

A List of Tiger Lily's Café® Mystery Series Books:

This cozy mystery series has everything you seek: an eclectic cast of characters, a mystery or two, and diligent detectives on duty. The detectives just happen to be feline.

Tiger Lily's Café is set in a Midwestern town nestled into the coast of a Great Lake. The setting itself acts as a character, bringing the reader into the sights, sounds and smells of the small resort community of Chelsea.

Read the series in order, or read any book alone. While characters grown and change, each volume stands alone with a clear beginning and a clear end.

- Turtle Soup (2014)
- Boo! (2015)
- Phishing (2015)
- Holiday (2016)
- A Rock And A Hard Place (2016)
- Splash (2016)
- Chasing A Butterfly (2017)
- Pumpkin Squash (2017)
- Snowblind (2017)
- Hearts On Fire (2018)
- Morel Of The Story (2018)
- Dragon Fire (2019)
- Beach Bunnies (2020)
- Shipwreck (2020)

Kathleen Thompson

Kathleen Thompson

Cast of Characters

Humans

Annie Mack, with the help of her "kids" and a talented staff, owns and manages a bed and breakfast, a cafe and other businesses on the south side of The Avenue. She has lived in Chelsea for only a few years, but her ancestral roots to the town date to the Civil War era.

Annie's SASHET Rainbow: (sa SHAY) a model that assigns color to each core feeling. **S**adness is blue; **A**nger red; **S**care green; **H**appiness yellow; **E**xcitement orange; and **T**enderness purple.

For more information, visit Liberation Psychotherapy: www.libpsych.com/articles/sashet/sashet.html.

Austin and Angela live in another state. They are the parents of Chris and have not been supportive of his career in the Coast Guard or his choice of a woman. Annie.

Ben and JoJo are college students. They work part-time all over town, including most of Annie's businesses.

Boone is the person to call if you need anything: mowing, snow removal, landscaping, maintenance, preventative maintenance, and just about anything else. He is married to **Harriet (Hilly)**, who provides business cleaning services. His sons **Daryl** and **Donny** work for him. Their roots are in rural Appalachia, and they are so much more than people think.

Candice is the head waitress at Mo's Tap. A native of Chelsea, her long, thick, dark hair is the envy of most women who meet her.

Carlos is the manager and baker at Mr. Bean's Confectionary. He is a citizen of the US but was originally from Mexico. He supports his mother and younger sisters, who still live there. He is married to Isabel.

Cheryl inherited The Marina from her parents. It's a small deep water marina with basic amenities. Cheryl is married to Ray. She has known Annie since they were children.

Chris is Annie's special friend, although neither of them are ready to commit to a permanent relationship. He is the Officer in Charge of the Coast Guard Station. His stress relieving hobby is art. His sketches – in charcoal, pencil and pastel – are sold for charity.

Clara owns the flower and gift shop, Bloomin' Crazy. She is a citizen of the US, originally from Haiti, and has an ebullient personality. She keeps The Avenue decorated with fresh and silk flowers year-round.

Cookie probably has another name, but this is what he goes by. He cooks at Mo's Tap and learns what he can from Felicity at every opportunity. He's reticent at best, and he yearns to have his own restaurant. To keep him, Annie opened a fine dining restaurant, Bon Vivant Grille, on Fridays and Saturdays inside the Café.

Daniela is a former professional baker from Mexico. She has been a mother figure to Isabel, who is married to Carlos. She and her adult daughters, **Rosa** and **Valeria**, now live in Chelsea

Diana is the chief instructor at L'Socks' Virasana (Veer AHS ana). She is Mem's daughter. Diana left home right after high school and did not speak to her mother until her return ten years later. Their relationship, while tenuous, continues to grow stronger.

Felicity is the chef at Tiger Lily's Café. She is young, perky and extremely talented in the kitchen. She manages the Café, the upstairs catering facility and outside catering operations.

Frank recently moved to Chelsea to open an antique shop, Antiques On Main. He and Mem are in a relationship.

Gema recently moved to Chelsea to open Gema's Creations. There, she makes and sells unique jewelry pieces. She has space in the front corner of Antiques On Main.

George is the bartender and manager of Mo's Tap. He is a top-notch bartender and can be counted on to keep confidences. He is a volunteer with the local Coast Guard.

Georgia manages the kitchen at the Bon Vivant Grille on weekends, coordinates catering for the Café, and cooks part-time at Mo's Tap. Her father, **Fred Calendar**, comes to town on occasion to see her and her daughter Frederica **(Little Fred)**.

Geraldine was the leader of the "it" crowd in high school, and somehow, life didn't turn out quite as she expected. Everything Annie isn't – perfectly dressed, perfectly coiffed, and perfectly awful – Geraldine is more than a thorn in Annie's side. **Everett** is her on-again-off-again husband.

Ginger is the daughter of Pete, the Chief of Police, and Janet. She works part-time at L'Socks' Virasana. Because she moved to town as a teen (when her father retired from the Marine Corps), and because she is one of the few African American teens in town, she sometimes feels like an outsider.

Greg is a progressive realtor in Chelsea. His goal is to get the right property to the right owner, always moving Chelsea forward.

Gwen is Annie's accountant. A motherly figure, her financial acumen is hidden from all but those lucky enough to have her in their corner.

Hank is a former member of the Town Council. He opposes Annie in every way.

Harry is the regular driver for the rental company used almost exclusively by folks on The Avenue.

Henrie manages the KaliKo Inn in an elegant manner. He does not invite confidences and speaks little about himself. Always formal in tone, people have difficulty pegging his accent. Is it French? Cameroon? Rwandan?

Holly and Jolly, twins, own DoubleGood, an electronics and hardware store. Holly lives in a wheelchair. Natives of Chelsea, they used to hate the names given them by their parents. Now, they enjoy the novelty of it.

Ian is a childhood friend of George. He coordinates local sporting and team events. He is light-hearted and fancy-free.

Isabel is married to Carlos. She is attending classes to become a citizen. She works with Carlos in the bakery and at Bon Vivant as the hostess.

Janet is Pete's wife. She spent twenty years as a Marine officer's wife. She traveled the world and is now living in Chelsea. She is an outsider, not having grown up here like Pete. She is the ultimate community volunteer.

Jennifer and Marie, sisters and nurse practitioners, own The Drug Store and The Clinic. Folks call the sisters before calling nine-one-one. Chelsea natives, they know everyone. And their secrets.

Jenny is an attorney who focuses on family law. She enjoys taking on cases that will right an injustice. She is always ready to engage in battle with those who don't believe a woman, much less a woman of color, can dance with the big boys.

Jerry learned how to make candy in a minimum security federal prison. He was not an employee. Jerry works hard to overcome his shyness, particularly around women.

Jet is from Puerto Rico. He moved in with Holly and Jolly, taking up residence with Holly. He works at Sassy P's Wine & Cheese.

Jerry is the candy maker at Mr. Bean's Confectionary. He learned how to make candy in a minimum security federal prison. He was not an employee.

Jesus manages Sassy P's Wine & Cheese and also selects the wines. His family, famous vintners in the Napa Valley, owned, farmed and made wine for generations before California became a part of the United States.

Joan is a member of the Town Council. She opposes Hank in every way. Clara's pet name for her is "Joan of Chelsea."

Juanita is a reporter for the local newspaper. As every reporter on every small town paper, she also sells ads, develops and places the ads, does photography and…reports.

Laila owns Babar Foods. A traditional Pakistani, she is raising her children without the assistance of a husband. Her children are **James**, **Ava** and **Carl**, who lives with Autism.

Marco is a police officer in Chelsea. He is "second in command" because he was the only officer that didn't go off-kilter during a hostage situation. Marco prides himself on being one-hundred-percent-eye-talian-American.

Martha used to own a bed and breakfast. The cottage was renovated to add an apartment suite, now occupied by Georgia and Little Fred. Martha is retired and enjoys spending time at the Inn.

Mem owns the health food store and cyber café, CyberHealth. Her wisdom is reassuring to everyone, including her daughter, Diana. She teaches the safe use of social media to all ages and has equipment and technology that is helpful to the small-town police department.

Minnie chooses perfect cheeses to accompany the rotating wine selections at Sassy P's Wine & Cheese. She comes from several generations of cheese makers in Wisconsin.

Nancy and Sam are Annie's mother and step-father. They have been married since Annie was a child. They come for extended visits in Chelsea and have learned to call this town their second home.

Pete is a native of Chelsea. He retired from the Marine Corps and is now the Chief of Police. Like Annie, his ancestors arrived in the Civil War era. His, however, came up via the Underground Railroad. He and his wife Janet have three children, the eldest of whom is Ginger. Clarice and Tamara are in high school and junior high.

Ramon (ra MONE) is Clara's boyfriend. A Jamaican by ancestry, he plays saxophone with a jazz fusion band called Bergamasco (after the breed of his dog). He and Clara work hard to maintain their mostly long-distance relationship.

Ray owns and operates The Escape, a yacht fashioned into a cruiser for fishing, diving and pleasure. He is married to Cheryl; Chris is his best friend.

Teresa is a newcomer to the area. She came to this community to serve. She pastors a small church, Soul's Harbor, and pastors the community through her outreach.

Terrence & Jerald Timmer-Schmidt have just moved to town. Terrence is a heart surgeon; Jerald is a psychiatrist. They have opened a medical office building in town.

Trudie is the barista at Tiger Lily's Café. She is from Jamaica and ended up in Chelsea when a former boyfriend dumped her at the campground. Felicity saved her, and they have been the best of friends ever since.

WQVX Channel Two. "The Lake Region's good news station" is anchored by **Charles Veritone**. The "ace on-site reporter" is **Dan Tapper**. **Felix** does weather.

Annie's Cats

Annie has seven cats. Most people would call them "rescue kitties." From Annie's perspective, each of them rescued her.

Tiger Lily is a beautiful tabby cat with soft green eyes. She is the titular manager of Tiger Lily's Café, the main gathering place for Chelsea. She is generally calm and logical.

Little Socks is a bright-eyed black cat with white socks. She has a commanding personality and is small and sneaky enough to serve as a cat burglar. She spends time at the yoga studio, L'Socks' Virasana (Veer AHS ana).

Kali, Ko and Mo are litter mates. They shared a secret language as kittens; Kali and Ko now speak "cat," but Mo still speaks "secret." Kali and Ko can be found at the KaliKo Inn, a lakeside bed and breakfast. Mo spends time at Mo's Tap, an upscale blues bar.

Sassy Pants is aptly named; it's difficult to keep this little girl's attention. She is overly sensitive and will react out of emotion instead of reason. She entertains at Sassy P's Wine & Cheese.

Mr. Bean is the baby of the family and is mostly gray with traces of tiger. He has two speeds: fast and love me.

Other Companions

Brown Mousie finds Sassy Pants and makes a new friend. He lives in the long building and roams from the Café to the Wine & Cheese shop. He stays primarily at Sassy P's.

Claire is a blue point Himalayan cat whose human is Frank. She's beautiful and loves people. She is stand-offish with other cats.

Cyril is an English setter whose human is Pete, the Chief of Police. Cyril is friendly and calm. He is an excellent hunter.

Daryll is a multi-colored tabby cat with an air of perpetual confusion. He lives at the state park. His human is the manager.

Fiamma is a Bergamasco. Dreadlocks cover her face. In fact, her entire body is covered with a combination of long dreadlocks and mats of hair. She is an outrageous flirt.

Honey Bear is a large, golden, long-haired mutt of a cat who believes it is his perfect right to be anywhere. Other cats hate him.

Jock is a Portuguese water dog whose human is Ray, the captain of The Escape. Jock is spirited and affectionate; he loves children.

Oscar McMurphy was a stray, named Scaredy Cat by the kids. Despite the name, she is a girl who now lives with Holly and Jolly. She claims Holly as her very own. She is often in and out of the Inn and other places on The Avenue with her brother, Simon Finnegan.

Simon Finnegan was a stray, named Fat Cat by the kids, who now lives with Holly and Jolly. He claims Jolly to be his mom. He is often in and out of the Inn and other places on The Avenue with his sister, Oscar McMurphy.

Speckles is a tortoise shell cat, named for her orange speckles. She belongs to Georgia and is Little Fred's chief nanny.

Tillie came to live on The Avenue with her dreadful family from England. She is a Jack Russell Terrier and now lives with Carlos and Isabel above the Confectionary. She has free run of The Avenue, including the Inn. She is small enough to squeeze in and out of the cat doors.

Guests at the Inn

The **Palindrome Gals** are in for the OktoberFest. **Hannah** is a face painter. **Anna** and **Eve** sell jewelry from Nepal. **Nan** and **Emme** have a bookstore. Both are authors. Nan writes cozy mysteries and Emme writes romances.

Bergamasco, a jazz quintet, includes **Ramon** on saxophone. Other combo members, in town for the OktoberFest, are staying at the Inn. They are:

- **BeeBop** – Guitar. Unhappily single. No woman will have him.
- **Jules** – Trumpet. In a perfect marriage with Noelle.
- **Manny** – Drums. No one has figured him out. He comes on to everyone, goes home with no one. Trudie is infatuated with him.
- **Noelle** – Cello. In a perfect marriage with Jules.

Others In Town

Dennis, Mem's ex-husband and father of Diana, has a cabin at the campground.

Harrison Jones, Diana's ultra-rich boyfriend, is in town and is staying with Diana in the home she shares with Mem.

Local Bullies: The same age as James and Laila, they either recently graduated from high school or stopped attending due to incarceration or choice. They are: **Billy**, the leader, **Dallas**, **Justin**, **Marc** and **Porter**.

Kathleen Thompson

Focus on what matters.

1

Monday morning wasn't lookin' good. Annie walked up The Avenue with her kids – most of them, five of her seven rescue cats – as they made their way to "work." A gray mist clung to everything. The October morning was chilly and drizzly.

Sassy Pants skittered to a halt at the door of Sassy P's Wine & Cheese, looking back at the unusual sight.

Mr. Bean lingered in front of Mr. Bean's Confectionary. As he looked at the strange thing, he was almost run over by a customer, who was leaving while eating a cream cheese Danish.

Mo looked not only at the thing on the street, he looked up and down to see if others were there as well. Seeing nothing more, he turned and went through the cat door to Mo's Tap. The blues bar would open for business in a couple of hours.

Little Socks, on her way into L'Socks' Virasana, the yoga studio, walked to the offending sight to take a sniff or two of large rubber tires.

Tiger Lily recognized the truck. She ran into Tiger Lily's Café and headed for the kitchen to tell Felicity to take care of it.

Annie followed Tiger Lily into the kitchen. "Felicity, did you know a delivery truck is taking up five parking spaces?"

Felicity, the manager and chef of the Café, threw a plate on the serving counter. Very un-Felicity-like.

"Yep. He can't get in the back."

The delivery man pushed a cart through the kitchen and said to Annie, "You need to clean that mess up."

Annie walked through the kitchen door to the alley, Tiger Lily on her heels. George and Candice, instead of getting the bar ready to open, had a shovel and broom, cleaning up a sticky, stinky, awful mess. Jesus, from the winery, and Jerry, from the Confectionary, were also working on piles of garbage, strewn around the alley and into Annie's private park, in and out of mud puddles left from last night's rain.

The dumpsters for each business, usually neat and behind privacy fences, were on their sides in the alley. Apparently, the vandals weren't satisfied with the garbage that spilled from the overturned bins, heavy from a weekend of business.

The lids had been pried open, and they must have used hoes or rakes to pull the debris from the insides and deposit it outside. Everywhere.

Annie closed her eyes, looked down at her new shoes, and heaved a sigh. She picked up a shovel leaning against the wall of the Café and waded in. The drizzle continued and became the perfect description of her feelings.

By the time they had finished, just in time for the garbage truck to make its Monday morning stop – late – she was soaked. Pumpkin seeds dangled from her straight, graying hair, and spots of what looked like baked acorn squash or pumpkin pie dotted her new shoes. Her jeans looked like she had worn them for a week while wading through a muddy river, and her top, usually flowing and colorful, was wet, clinging to everything, and drably colored by whatever each eatery had served the weekend before.

The trash men helped move the dumpsters back into place as they talked about the weekend vandalism.

"They musta waited 'til Sunday night, cuz nobody called us 'til taday."

"Yup. We's late getting' here cuz we been helpin' folks all over town get their stuff cleaned up. Thanks for havin' most of it done fer us."

"They's gettin' worst, that's fer shur. Las' week, we only had ta pick up rotten punkins and stuff like 'at. Taday, we's had ta git things put right, jus like here."

"Yup. It's gettin' worst, alright."

The garbage men finished and left, the truck lumbering down the alley. It was followed by two delivery trucks. The drivers looked agitated; they had waited for the alley to clear out so they could get to the bar and the winery.

Annie looked around. The humans helping were just as wet and dirty as she. Worse, she supposed. Five cats and one small dog sat a fastidious distance away from the stink. They remained under cover of the Café's second floor deck, "supervising" the operation. Dry and comfortable.

Annie shrugged at Tiger Lily, who seemed to think that perhaps the work was not yet done.

George put his shovel against the wall of the bar. "I'll get a hose and wash down the walls and garbage pads. Then I'll take a shower. Or two."

"I'll get one and start from this end," added Jesus. "Glad I live close. I couldn't stand myself if I had to get into a car."

This was not a typical day in Chelsea. Chelsea, a resort community on the sunset bank of a great lake, was generally quiet and peaceful or filled with the happy laughter of tourists. Not this. This was a side of Chelsea that Annie had not yet seen.

Annie lived on Sunset Avenue, known to most who lived here as just "The Avenue." She was a recent resident of the community. A few years ago, she inherited several businesses from her father. She moved from Chicago, leaving her old life behind, and embraced the life of a small business entrepreneur in this quaint lakeside town.

The town sprang to life during and following the Civil War, growing around the lumber industry. Later, after the harbor was excavated to allow for deep water access, Chelsea became a shipping center.

Annie lived in a Civil War-era house reminiscent of a southern mansion that was now a bed and breakfast. Situated on a white sand beach with lakefront access, the Inn was the largest and most prominent of the many B&Bs in the community.

Annie now stood behind a long, brick two-story building that was built to accommodate businesses that kept the lumber industry moving. Today, the businesses supported the tourist trade of the community. The second story was divided into several apartments rented by many of her management staff.

They paid a more-than reasonable rate, and Annie didn't have to worry about staff not being able to make it in through bad weather. It was a good deal all around. In fact, it was hard to tell who was getting the better deal, the renters or the owner.

Annie sighed again. "I'm going home the back way." She made her way down the alley and entered the yard of the B&B from the back of the Winery. Henrie, the B&B's manager, chief cook, bottle washer and toilet bowl cleaner, looked cool, clean, crisp and dry as he stood on the porch, watching her approach.

Henrie gave Annie a large, thick washcloth that had been soaked in warm water. Grateful, she rubbed it over her face and neck before cleaning her arms and hands.

"How did you know?"

Henrie handed over a thick bath towel. Annie dried her hair, face and neck and put the towel around her shoulders.

"Felicity sent a text and suggested I might want to 'clean you up a bit' before you tracked garbage through the Inn."

Henrie pointed to a pair of clean sandals waiting at the door. "Please remove your shoes."

Kali and Ko, the last of her seven cats, poked curious faces out the cat door; they sniffed the air around Annie. Evidently, they didn't like what they smelled, as they turned to run in the opposite direction.

"It was such a mess, Henrie. I didn't think to take pictures of it. Gosh. I should have called Pete."

"Felicity took care of that. She took photos this morning and sent them to Pete. Evidently, he and his officers were busy all morning."

"I suppose they don't have much to go on. I should put cameras back there. Oh, well. Nothing was damaged, really. They left a mess, but in the long run, we haven't suffered a loss. Just time. And dignity."

Annie pulled another pumpkin seed from her hair and threw it to the ground. "Maybe a pumpkin will grow there next year."

Henrie took Annie's offending shoes and placed them in a paper bag. "I will take these to the cleaner on my way out of town. Perhaps they can be salvaged. Too bad. This looks like the pair you purchased this weekend."

Annie nodded. "Who knew I should dress to sling garbage in the rain?"

Annie left the washcloth and dirty shoes for Henrie to handle as she went to the third floor and a long hot shower.

By the time Pete made it to the Café, the alley was clear, delivery trucks had been up and down a few times, all of the businesses were open and operating smoothly, and Felicity was once again her normal perky self.

Pete went to the service counter to talk to Felicity, but Cyril, his constant companion, sat behind the hostess stand to check in with Tiger Lily.

As Felicity handed over a cinnamon bun, Pete said, "You didn't sound so good when you called this morning."

I'm much better, since I didn't have to get out there in that muck. Did the pictures turn out alright, Pete?"

"Yes. They were quite vivid. I particularly liked the ones you sent later, the close-ups of Annie with pumpkin seeds dragging through her hair and a mound of something on her foot. What was that?"

"I think it was acorn squash. It was beautiful when it was served."

"It looked nasty on her shoe."

"They were new shoes, too."

"And you made her go out and clean while you stayed in to cook?"

"Pete, that's a no brainer. It didn't even come up in discussion."

"What was I thinking? Anyway, I have to interview everyone who lives upstairs. I thought I would start with you and Trudie. You live over the yoga studio. Did you hear anything?"

"My apartment is in the back, and all I heard was thunder. You can check with Trudie, but if I didn't hear anything, she probably didn't either. Unless she heard people walking down the street from the front."

Trudie was no help either. "I was up late on Saturday, so I was in bed really early last night. I didn't even hear the thunder."

As Pete and Cyril left, Trudie reached down to sneak a treat to Cyril.

Pete, over his shoulder and halfway out the door, said, "I saw that."

They went to Mo's, where Cyril said hello to Mo. He then went to the corner of the bar, stood and politely kept his feet to just the edge as Candice leaned over to give him a piece of jerky.

Pete watched and nodded to himself. "Why is it that everywhere we go, people give him food?"

"He's handsome, Pete. And we love him." Candice reached under the counter and pulled out another piece of jerky. "Do you want one?"

"No, thank you. Tell me what you heard last night."

George joined Candice at the bar. They lived in the larger, back apartment over Mo's. George said, "We didn't hear anything but thunder. We didn't even get out of bed to check."

At the Confectionary, Pete heard the same story. Twice. And Cyril got another treat. Cyril went to the window where Mr. Bean and Tillie danced. While he munched on his treat, Mr. Bean told him how silly Annie looked that morning.

Jerry lived in a small apartment over Mo's. "My apartment faces The Avenue. I heard thunder, and I got up to look out the window, but everything was quiet on the street."

Carlos and Isabel had the only apartment over Mr. Bean's. "Isabel and I came home late. We both heard thunder just as we were getting into bed. She looked out the north windows, and I looked out over the balcony. It was so loud, you know, and we wondered if something got hit by lightning. But we didn't see anything. It was dark, and the rain was pretty heavy."

Pete and Cyril walked next door to the Winery. Pete knew he wasn't going to hear anything else, but he had to complete his interviews. Cyril didn't get a treat at the Winery, but he went to the back room while Pete stayed in front.

Pete asked Minnie the same question. She and Jesus had lived in separate apartments above the Winery, but they renovated the area and now lived together in one large apartment.

"Pete, we didn't hear a thing last night but weather. It got loud, but it didn't seem unusual."

Jet walked through, carrying a case of wine.

"Did you hear anything, Jet? You live across The Avenue, but…"

"No, I didn't even hear the thunder. We were out on the deck last night until it started to rain, and I heard what sounded like some loud talking, but our deck faces the opposite direction. I think it was coming from the other side of Main Street."

"We had some activity over there last night. What time was this?"

When Pete finished his interviews, he looked around for Cyril. "Where is he?"

"He's probably in the back with Sassy Pants. She's back there a lot anymore. I think we have a mouse."

Pete walked to the back room and found Cyril and Sassy Pants looking at the base of a potted tree. Both started when he approached. If it was possible, Sassy Pants looked guilty.

Pete came close and examined the tree, finding nothing. "Minnie thinks you have a mouse, Sassy Pants. Can't you catch him?" Sassy Pants fled to hide under a hyacinth. Pete shook his head. "Come on, Cyril. We need to go to the Inn."

Pete saw Annie on the second floor landing as he entered. She was cleaner than she had been in the photographs, and he trusted she smelled better as well.

"I'll be right down, Pete. How about coffee?"

"Nothing for me, thanks."

"Treat for Cyril?"

"He's added two pounds since we hit The Avenue. He doesn't need anything more."

Cyril huffed and went into the library to look for Kali and Ko. Annie closed the computer and walked downstairs. Pete opened his phone and showed Annie the pictures Felicity sent. Of her.

"Can you delete those?"

"Nope. Going to hold onto them. They might come in handy. I have to ask, did you hear anything? See anything?"

"I know you have to ask. No. I didn't see or hear anything. Do you have any ideas about who is doing this?"

"Yes…but we won't discuss it now. Did you ever consider cameras back there?"

"I'm going to talk to Holly and Jolly today."

"Good. And if you get them, I'd like access to the monitors in case anything happens."

"Not a problem, Pete."

"Do you need a report for the insurance company?"

"No. We didn't have any damage. Just time."

"I should talk to Henrie, too. I know his apartment is nowhere near the damage, but he might have heard something."

"You can't talk to him today, Pete. We're between guests, so he left late this morning and won't be back until sometime tomorrow."

"Where'd he go?"

"You know Henrie. I don't ask, and he doesn't tell."

2

James drove his small car from Marsh Haven toward Chelsea. Ginger was with him; they shared rides to and from community college several days each week.

James lived on The Avenue, across from the Inn and Annie's other businesses. His mother and Annie's best friend, Laila, owned a grocery store. Laila and her three children lived above the store.

Ginger worked part-time at the yoga studio. Her father, Pete, was the Chief of Police.

They shared a deep friendship born from being outsiders in a small community. James was a newcomer and Pakistani. Ginger and her family moved to Chelsea when her father retired from the Marine Corps, making her a newcomer as well.

Pete had grown up in Chelsea. Then, less so now, African-American families were on the margin of society. Ginger was both a newcomer and an African-American in a small, midwestern community. Outsider.

James shook his head as he broke a long silence. "You and I both know who's doing this. They'll never be caught."

"They're too smart. And too mean. They're our age, out of school, and they still live at home without jobs. The only thing they know how to do is 'bully.'"

"Maybe we could tell your dad?"

"And what's he going to do? He arrests them all the time for petty crap, but short of following them around every night, I don't know how he'd catch them."

"Maybe we can do something."

"What?"

"I don't know. Maybe, well, okay, they'll be setting stuff up at the town park and on the beach for this weekend. If they want to make a real mess, they might do it there. We could take our sleeping bags out there and watch for them. Call it in if they show up."

"We need to study for our mid-terms."

"We can take our stuff out there."

"I don't know, James. We'd be out in the open, just begging for a fight."

"There are several places in the park that are kind of hidden. We could set up right by the community building. We could see both the park and the beach."

"Let's talk to Holly and Jolly first, see if they have something we can use to take pictures. Then we can stay hidden, maybe, and take the pictures to Dad."

Instead of dropping Ginger at her house, James drove straight to The Avenue, parking behind his mother's store. They walked in through the back door, straight out the front, hung a right and went into DoubleGood, the combination hardware and electronics store owned by twins Holly and Jolly.

Jolly stood as they walked in. She had been on her hands and knees plugging a new security display into an electric console. "Hi, kids. What's up?"

"Well," started James, "we wanted to talk to you about borrowing a camera."

"A digital camera?"

"One that can be used in the dark."

"That doesn't flash," added Ginger.

"What do you want to use it for? I mean, I kind of have to know to give you the right kind."

James looked at Ginger. She nodded for him to continue. "Well, we have this school project, and we have to take pictures of animals and things in the dark."

"Animals and things?"

"Well, you know, the kind of creatures that roam around in the dark."

Jolly put her hands on a shoulder of each teenager, turned them around, and pushed them in the middle of their backs until they reached the office.

"Sit," she said.

They sat.

James knew what was coming next, and it wasn't going to be good.

"What are you up to?"

James put a hand on Ginger's arm. He would take this. "It's like this, Jolly. We think we know who's doing this stuff around town, and we think they'll go where the OktoberFest is setting up."

"You know who it is?"

"Just a suspicion. Do you remember those guys that we all had trouble with last year? You know, the father of one of the guys mugged Annie."

"Yeah. Aren't they all out of school now? Are they still in town?"

"Yeah. They are. They didn't get jobs, didn't go on to school, they still just hang out, usually over by the box stores or over at that rough marina."

"Who are they?"

"Well, there's Billy, he's like the head bully ..."

Ginger added, "Dallas and Marc. They're pretty mean. Justin isn't as bad, most of the time, but he's not that good, either."

James finished. "And the little follower. Porter."

Jolly looked at Ginger. "Have you talked to your dad about this?"

"No, not really. I mean, we don't know anything for certain. We just think they could be doing it."

"Didn't they go to jail for something?"

"Two of them did, but they were still kids. They got out as soon as they turned eighteen."

"Why'd they come back to Chelsea?"

"Where else could they go? They're living with their folks, free rent."

"But your dad could keep an eye on them."

"He does. You know, part of the stuff they did involved me." Ginger winced, remembering the vile nature of her last encounters with the bullies. Fortunately, they had not been able to go through with their plans, which included grabbing her, ripping off her clothes and taking photos to send around on social media.

"Oh, yes. I remember now. Mean guys. Frankly, I don't want to help you put yourself in harm's way."

The teens sighed, but they knew better than to argue.

"Thanks anyway, Jolly."

As James and Ginger left, Jolly watched, hoping they would have the sense to stay as far away from those bullies as possible.

James and Ginger had other ideas. They started a plan to watch the town park at night. James didn't want to, but he acquiesced as Ginger said, "Not tonight. Let's get one good study night in first."

Billy carried a bag from the box store and walked through the rundown marina. He was on his way to a boat he called his second home. As he walked through the marina – which looked more like a junkyard than a working boatyard – he heard two loud male voices.

He stopped walking so he could hear more clearly.

One voice, he thought it was Mr. Cooper, the marina's owner, said, "That ex of yorn is one of the ritzy bitzy ladies of this here town. She's gotta have money. It don't matter that she said she don't. She got it, for sure. And she got rich friends, too."

"What are you saying? That I go ask her friends?"

Mr. Cooper laughed. Even to Billy it sounded cruel. "That ain't what I meant. I meant that if you put the screws to Mem, they'll come through for her."

Billy heard enough. He started walking again. As he got past the boat that had shielded him from view, he waved and nodded, but kept walking. He thought he recognized the other man. When he was real young, he used to see the man at his house. His old man used to work deals with several men, and he thought this was one of them. If he thought hard enough, he'd come up with the name.

There was only one woman in town named Mem. That smarty pants that was always coming to school to teach "social media safety." As if.

That witch with a "b" helped send him to juvie.

Billy hoped she had to pay and pay hard. And that gave him an idea.

He reached his own boat, climbed up and went down to the cabin. His crew was already there. Billy opened the cooler and pulled out a beer. His dad was pretty fly to buy it for them, but he was beginning to get on him about the money.

"My old man says we ought to be out making money for our beer. He don't believe me that we're lookin' for work."

"Yeah. We're lookin' for work, all right," said Porter. He looked to Billy for approval as he said it. Billy ignored him.

Porter rubbed him the wrong way. He had his good points. Like this boat. Porter found it and got an agreement from Mr. Cooper for them to use it. But usually, Billy didn't like him. No particular reason. Just didn't like him.

Billy looked around at his crew's expectant faces as the plan came together in his mind. "Whadaya say we go out again tonight?"

"They're gonna be watchin' for us," said Justin.

"No they ain't. We always done it on Sunday night. They won't look for us tonight."

"Where we gonna hit?"

"Earlier, I was thinkin' the school. Now, I'm thinkin' the front of one of them big buildings on Sunset Avenue. Them long ones."

"The front? Man, people will see us do that."

"Not if we wait till two or three."

"That bar might still be open."

"Nah. They close at one during the week. Nobody will be around."

"But what we gonna do to the front?"

Billy opened the bag and showed the contents to his crew.

"Spray paint? We're gonna paint it?"

"Man, that Annie has friends in high places, if ya know what I mean. We'll get caught fer sure."

Billy said, "We hit the place across the street. You know. There are those women who pretend to be doctors, and that crip in a wheelchair."

"Yeah, and that nerd's family from – where are they from again, Billy?"

"Some towelhead country."

"Yeah. And that witchy woman who preaches about 'cyber safety.' She helped send us up last year."

"And that nee-grow with an accent, always wears a flower in her hair."

"And the preacher lady."

By now, Billy knew he had them. They had warmed themselves up to the excitement of the evening. Except maybe Justin. He looked at the floor a lot, and didn't say much of anything.

Dallas said, "We need some rotten eggs and crap, too."

Porter knew the answer. "We can find that – and rotten tomatoes and other stuff – behind that box store on the east side of town. They put stuff that's almost rotten out back on Mondays and poor people come by to pick it up. They leave the worst of it behind. We can take a couple-a wagons from over yonder – there's a wheelbarrow over there, too – and pick up what's left. We can go just after dark."

Billy nodded. There was a reason to keep the nerd around.

Justin was between a rock and a hard place. Of all the bully boys, his family was the only family of substance. Professionals, Justin's father worked at an accounting firm in Marsh Haven, and his mother worked as a loan officer at the local bank. An older brother recently graduated from engineering school and a sister was in medical school. The parents were perplexed at the continued inexplicable behavior on the part of their youngest child, and, increasingly, so was Justin.

He could have had anything he wanted. A stellar high school experience, including sports. A college of his choice. But no. For whatever reason – Justin couldn't explain it to himself, much less his parents – he had tied his star to Billy and his band of bullies. And now, the bullies were getting meaner and resorting to violent actions.

He had never been attracted to girls before. They were just a means to an end, something to use to impress his gang members, either with a perceived liaison or with mean photographs. While Justin had not personally participated in a hateful social media campaign during their senior year, it wasn't for lack of trying. He was just lucky enough to not catch up to his target and take the pictures. Lucky. Yep. That was him. One lucky guy.

And now that he had seen someone to whom he could be attracted, she was a part of that crowd that hung out on The Avenue. Surely, someone would tell her about him, and his chances with her would be lost.

He was going to have to figure a way out of this mess.

3

As sometimes happened on Mondays – it was rare, but it did happen – the Inn was in between guests.

Tiger Lily and her siblings were painfully aware of this as they gathered underneath the tablecloth in their "agency," the table marked with a sign that said "Nine Cats Detective Agency."

The table was in the large dining room of the Inn, to the side of the door leading to the kitchen. It was rarely used for guests and instead functioned as a gathering place for felines and canines.

The tablecloth reached to the floor, and underneath the table were several cushions that were perfect for cats and small dogs.

Today they were joined by Fat Cat, Scaredy Cat and Tillie. Fat Cat and Scaredy Cat were the names given to the two cats when they were strays. They now lived in a fur-ever home with Holly and Jolly, with human-given names of Simon Finnegan and Oscar McMurphy. Tillie was a Jack Russell Terrier that lived above the Confectionary with Carlos and Isabel.

The reason they were painfully aware that no guests were present? Henrie didn't make a snack! He only did that for guests, and he graciously shared with the companions when he did. Sometimes, even though he was nice as he could be, he forgot all about the cats when he didn't need to prepare a snack for guests.

Sometimes, like today, he actually left the house to do something fun. Human fun, that is. Kali explained, *"He went to the city to see an afternoon movie, and he's going out to dinner there, too. Meeting some kind of friend or something."*

"I didn't know Henrie had friends," said Mr. Bean.

"Sure he do. He gots lots of friends," said Sassy Pants, whose grasp of the English language was a little loose.

The cats and little dog chatted among themselves, banter going from one to another.

"He never brings his friends here."

"That's because he's private."

"Wot's private?"

"He keeps his personal business to himself."

"Henrie has personal business?"

"Sure he does. All humans have personal business."

"But, what does he do when he isn't here?"

"We don't know."

"Why don't we know?"

"Because he's private."

"Does Mommy know?"

"I don't think so. She used to ask him stuff, but he didn't want to answer, so she stopped."

"But what if Henrie needs our help sometime? How will we know where he is? Or what he's doing?"

"We won't. He'll be on his own, unless he's here and needs our help."

"Kali and Ko, does he ever talk to you?"

"Not about his private stuff."

"Will we ever know?"

Tiger Lily put a stop to the conversation. *"Quiet now. There is no need to pry into his life. If he wants us to know anything, he'll tell us. Now, let's talk about today."*

"What a mess!"

"Ick!"

"Stinky!"

"Trill!" This comment was from Mo, who had never graduated from speaking the private language of kitten to speaking cat. His litter mates, Kali and Ko, generally had to translate. In circumstances like today, what he actually said didn't really matter, so no one offered a translation.

"Did anyone learn anything?" asked Tiger Lily. They took it upon themselves to be the guardians of The Avenue. Any information that one could gather about wrong-doing was important for all to know.

"Mommy really smelled bad when she got home."

"She was in the middle of it, shoveling it up and throwing it all back in the dumpsters. It got pretty messy."

"I heard Henrie and Mommy talk about it later. They said stuff like this has been happening all over town."

"I couldn't smell any particular human back there. Could anyone else?"

Cats and a little dog shook their heads in the negative. Oscar McMurphy said, *"Holly and Jolly put cameras behind our place, so if they do anything there, we'll see who did it."*

"Mommy should put cameras back behind our places."

"Maybe they know to stay away from cameras."

"Maybe, or maybe they're just stupid people and they won't see the cameras behind our place."

"But who knows if they'll go there? They may go somewhere else, like, I don't know. Somewhere else."

The conversation ended on a sad note. No information to share. No snack to eat. Nothing to do but curl up and take a nap.

They slept until Annie called them to the apartment for supper. Seven cats ran upstairs; a little dog and two large cats walked out the front cat door and to their respective homes for supper of their own.

4

Annie cuddled with the kids for a while before leaving for Sassy P's. Tonight, she would host a wedding reception for Carlos and Isabel. They married in a small civil ceremony some months ago, but circumstances prevented their friends from gathering in celebration.

Because they had to wait, they had more than a wedding to celebrate.

Carlos, an American citizen, had made a desperate trip to Mexico to untangle his mother, Daniela, and two sisters, Rosa and Valeria, from the clutches of a brutal gang. Now, Daniela and her adult daughters were going through the process of becoming citizens as well, and they had the requisite paperwork to live and work in America.

Isabel and Daniela both worked at the Confectionary for Carlos, and Isabel also worked as a hostess for Annie's fine dining restaurant, open on Friday and Saturday nights.

Rosa now worked as a receptionist for two doctors who were relatively new to town, Terrence and Jerald Timmer-Schmidt, a heart surgeon and psychiatrist, respectively.

Valeria, who had fallen in love with Clara's flower shop business, now worked as a counter assistant and design specialist. Bloomin' Crazy was one of the shops on the other side of The Avenue.

Valeria brought one of her skills to bear for this reception. Annie gazed around the Winery in wonder. It was filled with colorful origami butterflies. There were plain ones of blue, red, green, yellow, orange and purple.

There were butterflies in polka dots, paisley, starburst, geometric patterns and plaid. There were big ones, little ones, medium ones, individual ones, two and three connected together.

Butterflies sat on the tasting bar, on all of the tables, in the potted plants, on the display shelves, in the wine racks, in the cheese coolers, on the floor for cats to bat around, and even on the chairs.

Annie couldn't help but think of Tiger Lily and her fascination with the late summer monarchs just a couple of months ago.

Annie opened the celebration by introducing the couple, who needed no introduction. "I have the honor of presenting – for the first time in a formal setting – Carlos and Isabel, husband and wife. You have welcomed both to Chelsea; you are in great measure a reason for the success Carlos has had as a businessman and a baker. They now invite you to celebrate this blessed union with them."

After a champagne toast, Annie left the couple to circulate. Chris, Annie's "special" friend, was unable to attend, so she circulated solo, talking to everyone who came, which included almost everyone from The Avenue and around town.

She greeted Greg, a local realtor. With a hug, she said, "I've seen the house you found for Daniela and the girls. It's perfect! Just the right size for them and close to downtown."

"It has the best back yard in the downtown area, great for a vegetable garden, a front yard filled with flowers, three bedrooms and a large kitchen. It was perfect. I couldn't believe it when the house came on the market."

"And in their price range."

"Well, we had to work that out. Actually, Carlos bought the house. I'm sure they're paying him for it, and eventually, well, when the paperwork and red tape is taken care of, I'm sure the house will belong to Daniela. I tried to get a house for him, but he's happy where he is."

"If he wants a house, he'll buy it. Until then, I'm happy to have him and Isabel as tenants."

Annie saw a group of friends at a large table. She sat with them for a while. Clara was in the process of telling a story about the love of her life.

"Hi, Annie. You've heard this already." Clara turned back to the group. "So, anyway, Ramon said to this little woman, 'Hey, girl, you fine and all, but I got me someone. You can look, but don't touch.' And she said, 'Well I'm gonna touch me some of this anyway.' And he had to jump back behind BeeBop, but BeeBop didn't know what was happening, and he turned around and got a hand around his you-know-whats."

The group laughed. By now, they were familiar with all of Ramon's band members. Called Bergamasco, for the breed of Ramon's dog, they toured the country and were booked continually. They tried to take a week off – or at least four to five days – every month. Ramon spent his time off with Clara in Chelsea.

Clara continued. "You know, BeeBop doesn't get any of that, ever, because, I don't know. He gives off a vibe and no woman will have him. So he's pretty happy about the situation. He buys the woman a drink and she spent the rest of the evening trying to get away from him and into

Ramon's business. But Ramon, he's all over the room now, nowhere near her. Nuh uh."

Trudie asked, "So what's up with Manny? Does he have a girlfriend yet?"

"Honey, you need to look at someone else. I know you're attracted, but he is never going to do anything more than flirt with you."

"But he flirts so well...maybe some day...."

The women at the table laughed again, mostly with Trudie, rather than at her. She seemed to have a sense of humor about her unrequited love.

Annie sensed some tension between Mem and Diana but thought better of delving in. Instead, she asked, "Diana, did I see Harrison this evening?"

"Yeah. He got here late this afternoon, but he was pretty tired. He's taking a nap now, and might come over later. Or not. If not, he'll be there when I get home."

Diana met Harrison Jones when he came to Chelsea to do some ice fishing. A novice, he got himself into a little difficulty and had to be rescued. Throughout his visit, and later his recuperation in the hospital, Diana and he became very close. They now carried on a long-distance relationship. It didn't appear to be an issue with Diana, but Harrison belonged to the category of "filthy rich."

Mem added, "Neither Diana nor I wanted to miss this, and I have to admit, he's an amiable man. He didn't mind at all."

"I got lucky, Mom."

"You did."

The tension was still there. Annie could sense it, dense as a piece of sharp cheddar cheese. At least it wasn't over Harrison. But what? Annie could wait until they were ready to talk about it.

Felicity asked, "Where's Henrie tonight?"

"He had some free time – we're in between guests for a couple of days – and he's taking advantage of the opportunity."

"How? Where?"

"You know Henrie. I don't ask."

"You should. He knows everything about us and we know next to nothing about him."

"He likes it that way."

"And where's Chris?"

"Working." With a smile, Annie got up. "Need to circulate. See you later."

She sat next with Ray, Cheryl, Pete and Janet. As often happened in the evenings when they went out, their dogs were at the Inn, visiting the cats.

Pete, the chief of police, and his wife Janet had an English setter named Cyril. The same Cyril that received treats wherever he was on The Avenue.

Ray and Cheryl, owners of a cruise boat and the local deep water marina, had a Portuguese water dog named Jock.

Cyril and Jock were integral to the cats' success as "detectives" in town. Few humans knew of the special skills held by the cats and dogs, but everyone at this table did.

Pete asked, "What crimes have the kids uncovered lately?"

"Nothing. Everything is pretty darned boring right now."

"Good. You ought to get them going on this vandalism that's going on, though. You got hit pretty bad today. Worst I've seen."

"So I heard. It was very fun, cleaning it up. Not. Do you know who's doing it, Pete?"

"I think it's kids. Or rather, young adults. I'm keeping an eye on that group that's just out of school – you know who I'm talking about – but I haven't been able to catch them at it. So far they've eluded all the security cameras in town."

"I talked to Holly today and ordered cameras for the back of my places. I should have done that a long time ago."

"They probably won't be back, at least to your places. Frankly, though, they're running out of places to hit."

Ray said, "Maybe this is a run-up to Halloween and they'll quit then."

"Maybe. They are getting more destructive, though. They haven't damaged property yet – not really – and I hope that doesn't happen."

"They haven't come over to The Marina yet, or any of the lakefront businesses. At least, not that I've heard," added Cheryl. "Maybe we're next."

The evening went long. Everyone but staff had gone by the time Annie finished cleaning off the tables. Jet finally said to her, "Go home, Annie. We've got this. We're nearly finished anyway."

As Annie left, she filled a take-out bag with butterflies of every size, shape and color. Before going upstairs to bed, she went to the dining room, lifted the tablecloth and emptied the contents of the bag into the detective agency. Something to surprise the kids with the next day.

In the city, Henrie sat at a private table in the bar of his hotel. A tall, slender, elegant woman in a little black dress sat opposite him. They sipped pomegranate martinis, chilled just so, and enjoyed a companionable silence.

Jazz music played softly over a sound system and flames from lightly-scented candles danced on the tables. The house lighting was low; the air smelled of cherry blossoms. Their server was discreetly absent.

The woman spoke. "We don't get together often enough, Henrie. When was the last time?"

"It has been some time. Once again, I extend an open invitation to come to Chelsea. I have a lovely apartment. It would not match the ambiance of this place," Henrie looked around, "but we would be together."

"I'm not sure your Annie would know what to do with me."

"She is not 'my' Annie, and I am sure she would not have to do anything with you."

"You know what I mean."

"You must spell it out."

The woman paused. "Are you sure she's not in love with you, Henrie?"

Henrie smiled and looked down at his drink. "I believe anyone that knows both of us knows the answer to that question."

"Tell me again, Henrie. Make me believe you."

Henrie looked into her eyes. "I cannot make you do anything you do not want to do or that you cannot do. But I will tell you again. Annie and I most certainly love one another. We are not in love with one another."

"And you cannot imagine your life without her."

"That is correct."

"But I would be welcome."

"That is correct."

"And have you told your Annie about me?"

"I have not."

"Tell me again why you have not."

"I will not tell Annie about you until you are ready to introduce yourself."

"So it's my decision. You won't tell her until I do something."

"That, my dear, is correct."

"And tell me again about the other women in your life?"

Henrie smiled. "Their names are Kali and Ko...."

At that moment, Kali and Ko were up to their eyeballs in dog fur. To Annie, the evening was warm, but it was early fall. Most sane people were thinking about turning on their furnaces, or had already turned on their furnaces, or at the very least had closed their windows and doors to the brisk evening air. Annie had propped open the door

from her apartment that led to the third floor deck to
allow Cyril, Jock and the cats access to the smells of
autumn and the sunset.

Kali and Ko, big girls but the wimpiest of them all, had
snuggled into the side of one dog or another, while the
others kept their faces pressed to the railing. The last rays
of sun hit the water while they watched.

Tiger Lily asked Cyril, *"Does Pete know who messed up
the trash cans?"*

*"No. He knows who did it — you know, those bullies — but he
doesn't have any evidence."*

"What evidence does he need?"

"I'm not sure, but more than he has."

"Has he talked to them?"

*"Not yet. He's still thinking about it. The thing is, if Pete
doesn't have something that proves they were there, they'll get
their parents to lie for them and give them an alibi."*

"I can't imagine Mommy lying for us."

*"That's probably why you wouldn't do anything really bad.
You know your mom wouldn't cover for you."*

*"I guess. Don't you have to take a test or something to be a
mommy or daddy? You have to take a test to drive a car, or be a
citizen, or graduate from high school."*

*"You'd think that something this important would be the
same, but it's not."*

Tiger Lily sighed and fell into a fitful sleep against
Cyril's chest, until they heard Pete and Ray at the
apartment door. The big boys left with their humans, and

the cats trudged off to sleep in the dining room. Their mommy was still at the winery.

5

Kali and Ko reached the kitchen first on Tuesday morning. They missed Henrie and couldn't wait for bacon treats. There was no Henrie. No bacon smell. Nothing.

The girls ran to his apartment and through the cat door. He wasn't home. They hung their heads, and in utter dejection, they slowly made their way to the steps leading up to the apartment.

Tiger Lily and the rest of the family ran down the stairs and nearly bowled them over.

"What's wrong?"

Kali and Ko answered at the same time. *"No Henrie."* *"No bacon."*

"What?" *"Trill!"* *"No!"* *"Wot's wrong?"* *"Henrie's not here?"*

Annie followed them down, stopping near the bottom of the steps, unable to continue because of the cat conference. "Come on, kids. Let me down."

Tiger Lily lifted a plaintive face to her. *"Henrie's not here!"*

"I don't know what you're saying, Tiger Lily, but come on, let me down. We need to get to work."

"But we need our bacon."

Annie seemed to sense their dismay. "Henrie stayed over in the city last night. He figured you kids could get by for one day without bacon. Come on. You can all come to the Café first and get a treat from Trudie."

"Us too?" asked Kali.

Annie, again almost reading their minds, said, "Kali, Ko, come on. You can get a treat at the Café, too."

They left, running over themselves in their haste to get through the cat door to the next best morning treats, those handed out by Trudie at the coffee bar.

Annie followed more sedately. Once out the door, she nearly tripped over the cats again. They were stopped, staring across The Avenue. Annie looked as well.

"Oh, no. You kids go on to the Café. I'm going across the street."

The cats ran across the street.

Annie shook her head, knowing they had to find out what was happening.

The cats were greeted by Fat Cat and Scaredy Cat. They stood with Cyril, surveying the damage from the relative safety of the median.

"Look at this mess! We all thought they would go behind the building. Holly and Jolly put cameras up. On the back! Not on the front! So we don't know who did it!"

Annie went straight across to The Clinic and The Drug Store first. Marie and the office staff were shoveling rotten pumpkins, tomatoes and eggs off the sidewalk while Jennifer hosed down the two storefronts.

"They got us good. This time they used paint. Look."

Spray paint, not the usual Halloween-fun soap, had been taken to the windows, which, for these nineteenth century buildings, took most of the wall space. And of course, the paint over-splattered to the painted brick walls and the painted logos. Taunting words had been used.

Misspelled, but used. The only words spelled correctly seemed to be the four-letter variety.

It looked as if some of the rotten vegetables and eggs had been thrown before the paint and some after, leaving lots of debris embedded in the dried paint.

"We're going to have to repaint everything. It's the same all the way up to the corner."

Annie stood back and looked. They were right. All of the storefronts, each one painted a unique pastel color with logos carefully applied, had been damaged in the same way. Red, black, white, green and purple paint slashed angry marks, vile words and gang-style designs from The Clinic all the way to Soul's Harbor.

"Can I do anything?"

"No, Annie. Not a thing you can do. You cleaned up yesterday. Today it's our turn."

Annie walked up The Avenue, speaking to each of the business owners in turn. She took some extra time with Holly and Jolly, counting mounting areas and adding to her order of surveillance cameras.

She stopped to talk to Pete as he took photographs of the damage. "I ordered cameras for the back yesterday, but just now I added cameras for all of The Avenue. They'll cover the front of the buildings and the median as well. They haven't touched that, yet, so…"

"It looks like whoever it is has stepped up their activity. It used to be on weekends. Now…well…this was the second night in a row. And it looks like they're going to concentrate on this part of town. I'll put an officer on patrol starting tonight, but, you know, I don't have a lot of staff."

"We're counting on you to catch them, Pete."

"Uh huh. I'll get right on that. Come on, Cyril. We need to go."

Cyril seemed to end a conversation with the cats and trotted to Pete, ready to move.

Annie watched as her cats seemed to drift away, thoughts of a treat forgotten, to their own places of business. She had made it to the end of The Avenue and had spoken with Pastor Teresa. Soul's Harbor was the last of the storefronts. She had a mess on her hands, just like everyone else. Annie turned back to Babar Foods.

Laila and James had gotten the sidewalk and storefront as clean as they could – before repainting, that is – but Annie didn't see anyone in the store itself. She walked to the storeroom. Boxes were everywhere. There was barely room to walk through.

Annie raised her voice to be heard. "Hey, are you in here somewhere?"

"Here, Annie," called Laila. Annie followed the sound of her voice. Inside the storeroom and outside on the gravel parking lot were cases of canned goods. Annie had never seen so many in one place before. Not even at a big box store. As Annie watched, several cars pulled in, and people, mostly women, and most of whom were familiar to Annie, got out.

"We thought we'd come help, Laila," said a woman named Janice. Annie knew her to be active with the high school band boosters.

"Thanks, Janice. With our problems out front, we can use the help."

"Do you have a list? Who gets what? If you do, we can sort it out for you, and you can go on in and work the store."

"Thanks. I really appreciate this. James, stay here and help the women. I think we've saved enough boxes, and here," she reached into a deep pocket and pulled out a handful of permanent markers. "Use these to mark the boxes."

"Okay. Oh, you know, we're going to take all the labels off our cans. We'll mark the tops of the cans, so the food pantry will know what they're getting."

"Great. I'll leave it to you, then. Annie, would you mind giving me a hand in the store for an hour or so?"

Annie walked in with Laila, looking over her shoulder at James and the women as they sorted canned goods for... "What are they doing, Laila?"

"This was one of our blessings today. The delivery came early this morning, after those bully boys had done their damage, so we didn't have to clean that up as well."

Annie worked on the deli display, opening containers of salads and meat dishes, while Laila rotated the produce. They were the only ones in the store, so their conversation continued, sometimes with voices a bit raised, but still able to hear one another.

Settling in to her job, Annie asked, "But what are all the canned goods for?"

"Oh. They're for the CanStruction projects."

"The what?"

"CanStruction. For the OktoberFest. Lots of groups are in the contest to see who can make the best display. They decided what they would build, what colors they would need, and they ordered based on that. You know, if they wanted yellow, they got corn, red, tomatoes. Several groups ordered those colorful soda cans. So we have to sort them based on what they ordered. In the end, all of the cans will go to the food pantry."

"Where are they going up?"

"In the town park, in the community building."

"So, how do they do them?"

"Well, take Janice and the band boosters. She said they are taking the labels off, so they'll have silver cans. When she put in her order, she got several different sizes of cans, but she didn't care what I ordered. They're going to take their silver cans and make a skull. A lot of groups are doing Halloween things, since it's so close."

"How…"

"Oh. You really don't know about this? All of the projects will be at least six feet tall, some of them taller, and they have a twelve by twelve area to put up their display. So, well, I know one group is going to make a giant garbage can and put Oscar the Grouch in. You know, from Sesame Street. They're going to use cans and a lot of lime Kool-Aid packets for his head and arms. And they'll probably use some cans to make it look like he's spread garbage around."

"So they buy these cans…"

"And they have a contest. The judges will decide who won, but these groups, they don't have to pay an entry fee, because they bought all the food for the pantry. The judges are actually going to be from the pantry, so no one has to pay anyone."

"What do they win?"

"I think a ribbon. Or maybe a trophy. Or maybe just a sign. They'll get publicity just for participating."

"How did I not know this was going on?"

"You've been busy with other things, like the bands. You got them going, right? And the food?"

"And the beer. And wine. Yeah, I guess we've been pretty involved. I just didn't know about this."

"It's a good deal, especially for the pantry as we go into the holiday season."

"You know, the closer we get to this weekend and OktoberFest, the more I worry about these vandals. They have to know we'll start setting up soon, and that will just be like honey to a bee for them."

"I know. Did the committee hire security?"

"The committee talked about security, but not the ramped up kind we're going to need. I'll talk to Ian."

"Well, you don't need to go far." Laila jutted her chin toward the window. "Looks like he's looking for you."

Annie had finished the deli display, so she walked to the door, stuck her head out and called, "Ian, are you looking for me?"

Ian, the town's volunteer coordinator of sport and event festivals, was a favorite of Annie's kids. They loved the way he gave two-handed pets, lavishing complete attention on them for a few seconds whenever he saw them.

He was a favorite of Annie's also. He was a perennial bachelor and was often to be found in the company of one or another of Annie's short-term female guests at the Inn, usually of the attractive sort.

"I was. Can we talk about security?"

"You're reading my mind." Annie stepped back into the grocery store. "Are you good without me, Laila?"

"Go. I'm fine. Tell Ian hello, and take him an apple. He likes the Honey Crisp."

Annie picked up an apple and left.

Ian and Annie walked as they talked, up The Avenue toward the corner, where they would cross and go to the Café for coffee. And breakfast for Annie.

As they passed CyberHealth, Mem's tea shop and cyber café, Annie's eyes were drawn to the window. She saw Mem in deep conversation with a man she didn't recognize. As if drawn like a magnet, she glanced across the street. She saw Diana at the door to the yoga studio. She didn't seem to notice Annie, but she glared in the direction of Mem's shop.

Diana realized Annie had seen her. She ducked back into the relative safety of the yoga studio. Little Socks sat on a pillow in the window, gazing across The Avenue at the vandalized building. Diana sat next to her and ran her hand from head to tail, head to tail. Diana was one of the few persons allowed to touch the little black cat.

As long as it was Diana – or Annie – Little Socks settled into a purr for several strokes. As soon as the purr stopped, Diana knew it was time to take her hand away.

Harrison joined her, sitting on a bench backwards, facing the window.

"Is he still over there?"

"Yes. I don't know why he doesn't just go away. Mom's not going to give in. I hope she doesn't give in. Why does she talk to him?"

"She was married to him. And she has a child by him. That kind of bond doesn't disappear, no matter how strained it gets."

"I'm surprised he hasn't approached you." Diana sat up straight. "Did I tell him anything about you when you met?"

"No, you didn't. You didn't even give him my last name."

"Oh, thank goodness. I don't even know him anymore, but it seems like he'd put the pinch on you if he had a clue you had any money."

"He won't be able to tell from watching me. Or looking at that beater truck I drove this time."

Diana laughed. "I couldn't believe it when I saw it. You said you were driving a truck…"

"…I needed it for that desk. Frank has it ready for me."

"But you're driving a beater! Where's that expensive Platinum something?"

"In the shop. Mom's gardener let me borrow his."

"So you drove the run-down truck of 'the help' several hundred miles to pick up an antique."

"Don't get so worked up about it. He drives a truck that's almost as expensive as mine. This is the one he uses when he has to haul fertilizer."

Diana laughed again. Then she looked across The Avenue. The man was leaving the building. He looked across at the yoga studio and almost started across the street. He stopped, though, apparently sensing the futility, and walked down the sidewalk toward the state park.

Henrie packed the car carefully, then turned to say goodbye to his companion. "This was a lovely break. Thank you for fitting me into your schedule."

"Henrie, that's so formal. You know I would make time for you anytime."

"Then make time for me and come to Chelsea. I will show you the wonders of small town living. You can leave the rigors of restaurant management for one night, certainly. Perhaps two."

"But what do you offer, besides a day or two?"

"I would offer a lifetime."

"But in a small town."

"A small resort town with a large heart, and the capacity to add at least one fine dining establishment. There are opportunities…"

"I'm sure. Perhaps I'll investigate."

"Perhaps. Well, then, until next time…."

As Henrie drove away, missing her already, he considered what life would be like should he decide to make a change. Perhaps he was being stubborn. Perhaps he could find something satisfying in the city. He would consider the possibilities.

6

Annie stayed at the Café through the lunch rush. This was a perfect October day. Sunshine. Crisp, cool air. The smell of fallen leaves. The sound of the lake breaking against the beach as the water refreshed, changing from summer cool to winter warm.

This kind of a day brought the locals out in droves. Tourists were in town year-round, but this time of year, they tended to come on the weekends. Tomorrow, they would start to arrive for the OktoberFest, which would run Friday and Saturday.

Today, the gossip was all about the vandalism, and how it had started to center itself on The Avenue.

Annie had great friends in town. She also had a few detractors. Only a few, but a powerful few. They loved to use days like today to meet in Annie's businesses and talk trash within earshot of Annie and her staff.

Geraldine – that perfectly dreadful and perfectly dressed and coiffed woman with body parts augmented or condensed in several places – held forth at the Café, her favorite trashing place.

Geraldine was in high spirits. The court order prohibiting her from coming onto The Avenue had been lifted a couple of months ago, and she wasted no time reinserting herself into the mix. Annie and her staff had a new way of dealing with Geraldine, her husband and her friends. They were syrupy, sickeningly sweet, overly complimentary of Geraldine's hair, clothes, shoes, purse, make-up, anything they could think of, and tight-lipped about anything else.

At one point, when Geraldine and her husband were in an off-again portion of their relationship, Geraldine had tried to establish a relationship with Frank. Frank owned an antique shop on Main Street and was in a relationship with Mem. He had almost succumbed to Geraldine's attentions but pulled himself away in time.

As Annie watched Frank come in for lunch, she mused that it was a year ago this month that Frank had almost fallen. Today, he had only a polite hello for Geraldine as he made his way to a small table at a window.

Trudie handed Annie Frank's regular coffee order – he always ordered the monthly special - and Annie walked it to the table, taking a menu on her way.

Tiger Lily followed and jumped to one of her ledges, saying a special hello to one of her favorite customers.

"Here you go, Frank. Mexican latte. Cinnamon, cayenne and an extra shot of espresso."

"Perfect. Tell me again what your Mexican specials are this month."

Annie turned to look at the board, refreshing her memory. She turned back to Frank, who rubbed Tiger Lily's arching back while Annie talked.

Annie recited in perfect server-ese, "Well, sir, we have two special soups, chicken tortilla and creamy tomatillo, both spiced to perfection. Entree-sized salads are the chopped salad with honey-lime dressing – that has a bed of chopped romaine with tomatoes, jicama, corn, radishes, avocado, red bell peppers and black beans – and a mixed greens and quinoa salad with black beans, avocado, orange segments and orange lime dressing. We have two special sandwiches. The pelona comes on a fried bun and has shredded beef, lettuce, avocado, crema – that's a Mexican version of sour cream – and either a hot red sauce or a hotter green sauce. The chanclas is actually two small sandwiches with shredded beef, avocados and onions, smothered in a red sauce. Hot. Both in temperature and taste."

Frank stared at Annie. "You did that very well, Annie. You should consider becoming a server full-time."

Tiger Lily put her paw on the menu, indicating something that was served all the time at the Café.

Frank looked at the item, then at the cat. "Thank you, Tiger Lily." He turned to Annie. "I'll have your curried chicken salad with pecans and grapes on a croissant with a side of cottage cheese and whatever fresh fruit Felicity has back there. And the same to go for Gema."

Gema owned a custom-made jewelry business that was set up in the front corner of Frank's antique shop. They rarely left the building at the same time, working together to keep both stores going without hiring additional help.

Annie looked at Tiger Lily, who stared back. Annie sighed. "Frank, one of these days we'll take you on a trip to the spicy side of life."

"Maybe, but not today."

Annie walked the order to Frank's server and went back to his table. "May I sit for a while?"

"Sure. What's on your mind?"

"Mem. Is something going on with her?"

"What do you mean?"

"Oh, it just seems like she and Diana have something, you know, going on between them. Some tension."

"Oh. That. Well, there is a little something, but I don't want to get into it. Nothing that a little time won't sort out."

"Okay. Well, I shouldn't pry. But if I can do anything…"

"There's not a thing that anyone can do. But hey, let's talk about the big elephant in the room. Mem said you ordered cameras to go up all over The Avenue."

"Yeah. I said something to Jolly today, and she called her distributer. They had things on hand, and they'll be here this afternoon to install them."

"I ordered cameras myself today. Your large order must be why the distributer can't take care of me until next week."

"Did you order for both front and back?"

"Yes. Why not? You can't tell where they're going to hit, and either they'll catch whoever it is in the act or they'll scare them away."

"I'm sorry my order is holding yours up. Let's hope nothing happens on your block this week."

Frank's lunch order arrived and Annie excused herself to return to the coffee bar. Tiger Lily stayed, in the hope that some chicken salad would find its way to a spot on the table that was easy for her to reach. Frank was always a soft touch.

When Annie finally said good-bye to everyone at the Café, she started her trek down The Avenue. She stopped in at each of her businesses, giving some attention to each cat and making sure her staff had everything they needed.

On her way into L'Socks Virasana, she noticed cameras going up on The Clinic and The Drug Store. The workmen seemed to be pointing one at the median.

As she left the yoga studio and walked to Mo's Tap, the workmen were in the middle of the other side of The Avenue, placing cameras between Bloomin' Crazy and DoubleGood.

When she left Mo's and walked to Mr. Bean's, the installers were at Babar Foods.

When she left Mr. Bean's, they were putting up the last of the cameras on that side of the street, in between CyberHealth and Soul's Harbor.

Annie stepped into Sassy P's. Jet and Minnie were on either side of the tasting bar. The bar was filled with pumpkins of every size. The two seemed to be sorting the pumpkins into similar sizes and shapes.

"Pumpkin delivery came. You got a lot!"

"Yep. The bar in the back is full of them as well."

"Where are you going to put the people? And the wine?"

Minnie laughed. "We're going to move the pumpkins. Before we're done, they'll all be on tables in the back room, ready for people to choose."

"How many pumpkins do you have?"

Jet answered. "Over fifty people signed up, and we figured there would be walk-ins, so we went crazy. We got seventy-five."

"Seventy-five. Wow. That will be a big event. And in the middle of the week? Who knew?"

"We need to do things like this more often."

The "things like this" was a wine and pumpkin party. For a fee, men and women could come in, have a couple of glasses of the wine of their choice – and as much else that they wanted to purchase – and a pumpkin. Painting supplies would be available, and a local artist would lead participants through creative ways to paint a Halloween pumpkin.

The local artist would be Chris, Annie's special friend, the Officer in Charge of the local Coast Guard Station, and a talented water colorist, sketch artist and photographer.

"Are you going to do a pumpkin?"

Annie was pre-registered, but she hadn't decided if she would come for the pumpkin or just for the wine.

"I'll decide tomorrow." Annie reeled whenever she thought about people who tried to teach art to her in the past. To a one, they recommended, in essence, that she not quit her day job.

Annie spent a minute with Sassy Pants, knowing the little girl would head for home shortly after she walked out. When she got to the sidewalk and looked toward the town circle, she saw the installers. They were at the corner, putting cameras on the Café. They faced the side, on Main Street, the front, on The Avenue, and across, toward the median.

She decided they would probably finish today, but they still had the rest of this street, the Inn, and behind her businesses. As she considered this, she noticed another installation crew arrive. They must have come from other jobs and were now going to double-team Chelsea. Yes, they would finish today.

Annie crossed The Avenue to talk to Holly or Jolly about the installation of the monitors. She hadn't decided yet where to put the brains of the operation.

Billy was having a hard time waking up. Early this morning he crashed on the rundown sofa. Both of his parents were at work, his mom at the box store and his dad at a factory on the far side of town.

Now Billy's head was pounding, a combination of lack of sleep and too much beer.

Or maybe it was the door.

It was the door.

"Hold yer horses," he croaked. The pounding continued. "I'm coming!"

When Billy finally got to the door – why did his folks lock the darn thing anyway, there was nothing of value here – he saw the Chief of Police and another officer.

"What?"

"Do you remember me, Billy?"

Billy made a face and nodded his head in an act of stupefied wonder. "Yes, officer, I remember you. How can I help you, officer, sir?"

"May I come in?"

Back in Billy mode, he snapped, "No. Whadaya want?"

"I want to talk to you about some vandalism around town."

Billy sighed. "I didn't do it."

"Can you tell me where you were last night?"

"What time?"

"All night?"

"Right here, watchin' TV with my dad."

"And the night before?"

"Same thing."

"How about a week ago Sunday?"

"Same thing."

"What do you watch on Sunday nights?"

"How do I know? One day is the same as every other. I watch TV with him every darned night."

"Your father will verify that?"

"Yeah."

"And your mother?"

"What about 'er?"

"Will she verify it as well?"

"Well, she better verify it."

"Are they home?"

"Somebody's gotta pay the rent. They work."

"Tell me where, please."

Billy told them and slammed the door in Pete's face. He knew he didn't have to call his dad. He'd be cool. But he called the box store and waited until his mother came on the line.

"I was home all night last night and every other night, watchin' TV with dad, and that's what you're gonna say when they ask you."

His mother sighed and hung up the phone.

7

Tiger Lily and her siblings were alone this afternoon. No Fat Cat and Scaredy Cat. No Tillie. No Cyril or Jock. Just them.

As Tiger Lily trotted down the street toward the Inn, well behind the wiggling butts and wagging tails of the rest of the family, she wondered if Henrie had returned. Kali and Ko didn't come to the Café for treats, either this morning or early this afternoon. That meant – maybe – that Henrie had come home.

He was home! Tiger Lily entered the cat door to hear everyone talking to Henrie. She ran into the dining room and went straight to Henrie, standing tall to pat his thighs with her front paws.

"And Tiger Lily, it is good to see you. Now that you are all home, I will serve the treats."

Kali and Ko said, at the same time, *"Treats! Henrie has treats!"* *"We don't have guests, but Henrie made treats!"*

Henrie came back from the kitchen with seven little plates, each one containing some bacon, minced chicken livers, a tiny piece of mozzarella cheese and half a small green olive. Little Socks particularly appreciated the olive.

No matter how pleased they were to see Henrie, all concentration went to the snack, and for at least a minute, there was not a sound to be heard but chewing, swallowing and lip smacking.

While the cats ate and cleaned themselves, Henrie sat at the dining room table. Tiger Lily watched him watching them. He was happy to be home.

Tiger Lily politely thanked Henrie by going to his leg and reaching up to him. Henrie put his face low so she could pat his cheek.

"You are welcome."

Tiger Lily went to the detective table, nosed the tablecloth aside and stopped. There were butterflies! Everywhere! She jumped in, knocking several to the floor, and chased them around. The other cats saw what she was doing, looked under the table and did the same.

Before Henrie knew what was happening, there were butterflies everywhere. Probably twenty or so. Colorful origami butterflies. There were so many, the cats didn't need to fight one another over the best one. They were all beautiful.

When Annie got home, the cats and the butterflies were in the dining room, foyer, library, and down the hall headed toward the all-season porch.

"Henrie, it's so good to see you. The kids found the butterflies, huh?"

"Yes. Were these from the wedding reception?"

"Yeah. Pretty, aren't they? Can we let them hang around the house for a while?"

"I have no reason to lean down and pick them up. As far as I am concerned, they can stay until they fall apart."

Annie and Henrie talked to one another as they walked to the kitchen, and Tiger Lily gathered her siblings together.

"This is fun, but we have to talk. What did everyone learn today?"

Excitedly, they told one another everything they knew.

Cyril had smelled the bully boys.

Pete suspects the bullies, but he doesn't have any evidence.

Mommy got cameras for everywhere.

That may not help. Holly and Jolly had cameras behind the building, but they did their damage in the front.

People are worried about the town park with that big OktoberThing going on this weekend.

Ian and Mommy talked about hiring security people for the weekend.

Frank didn't tell Mommy what was going on with Mem and Diana, but something isn't right.

Diana's boyfriend is in town, but he isn't the problem.

People will be painting pumpkins at the winery tomorrow night.

This last bit was from Sassy Pants, to which Little Socks replied, *"What does that have to do with anything?"*

"She say wot duz we know, and dat's wot I know."

By now, they had run out of interesting tidbits to add to the conversation. One by one, they curled up under the detective table and went to sleep.

Henrie poured coffee and asked, "What happened across The Avenue?"

"The same group – probably – that's been doing vandalism all over town. But they've broken pattern. They did it for the second night in a row, and on a Monday, not a Sunday, and they've gotten more vicious and destructive."

"Rather. I assume the insurance company will pay for repairs?"

"Probably, but probably also with a big deductible. Maybe we can do something to raise money to pay that, or at least help."

"Good idea."

"Oh, and cameras are going up all over The Avenue. We'll have control of the monitors here, somewhere. I still have to ask Holly or Jolly where to put them."

"It would be convenient in the kitchen. Readily available to both of us but invisible to our guests. Perhaps in this cabinet above the computer."

Annie and Henrie looked at the cabinet. They took measurements, which Annie texted to herself. She would ask Holly or Jolly if it could work.

"Did you have a pleasant evening?"

"I did."

Annie didn't press. That was all she would get.

8

Annie had one final "meeting" with her management staff about the details for the weekend. As usual, if the meetings were not daytime skyping, they were nighttime fun. Tonight they met at Mo's Tap to have dinner and to try the margarita flights. Chris and Annie were the last to arrive. They joined the group at a large table in the back.

Annie looked at the special menu. She couldn't decide what to have, but she finally settled on the Mexican lime soup, with chicken, adobo sauce, avocado slices, cilantro, and – of course – lime, and Mexican coleslaw, which turned out to be the regular coleslaw vegetables topped with a dressing made with olive oil, lime, garlic, honey, cumin, oregano, coriander and hot sauce. "Whew!" she said to Chris. "Spicy!"

While they ate, Annie asked if anyone had questions or issues with the OktoberFest.

Felicity was still angry about Monday's vandalism. "You and Ian talked about more security, right? We're going to have equipment out there overnight on Friday, and maybe Saturday night, depending on how late we go."

"Ian is going to check his budget and talk with his security team. He'll add what he can during the weekend."

"That covers Friday and Saturday. What about Thursday? Lots of people will be setting up Thursday afternoon."

"He's going to cover what he can. He wasn't sure how far the money would go."

Annie asked about the keg toss. "So, will the kegs have beer in them?"

Most of the table laughed, while a few looked confused. George answered. "No. Empty kegs. We really only need one. Everyone that signs up gets three tries, and the longest toss is the one we use."

"So, what, they heave it from their shoulder?"

"They hold it by one of the handles, and they can throw one of two ways. They can swing it, you know, like a pendulum, and release it when it gets as high as it can go, or they can spin and swing it, more like a hammer throw."

"And you have enough room, for the ones that can't throw it in the right direction?"

"Plenty of room. We have about thirty pre-enrolled, but I figure we'll get several walk-ins. We have room for everyone to stand around and watch at the edge of a safe zone.

Chris asked, "When do you open up that keg and serve the free beer?"

"First thing! We open with that Friday at two o'clock. Free beer until it's gone."

"Two kegs?"

"One. And small glasses. We want everyone to have a little bit, but we need to raise money to pay our expenses, too."

Annie saw a man in a corner booth. He looked like the man she saw talking to Mem earlier in the day. She leaned over to George. "Know that guy?" She nodded her head in his direction.

George turned to look. "Oh. Yeah. That's Dennis. He's Mem's ex. He's staying at the campground. He's been in town a couple of days."

"Oh. I never met him."

"He left when Diana and I were kids. Just took off."

"Do you know anything about him?"

"Not much. We were in grade school when they got a divorce, and he never came to school events. He finally just left town when we were in junior high. Diana didn't talk about him. I think he worked at one of the orchards. Something tells me he might have gotten into some kind of trouble before he left town, but I don't remember what it was."

"If I remember the story correctly, Diana was mad at Mem for divorcing him, blamed her that he left town."

"That was an angry kid. Diana the adult knows better. She's not mad at her mom anymore. At least, not for that."

The conversation was interrupted by Candice and two other servers bringing trays of margarita flights. A flight went in front of everyone. Six small glasses on a wooden tray made to hold the glasses without slipping.

George became the host. "Okay. You have six short – I emphasize the short – chilled margaritas in front of you. If you order a regular size, you can get them on the rocks or frozen. This is the 'rocks' type, but the glasses are too small for ice. Only thinking of all of you."

"Thanks, George."

"Yeah. You're a great guy." This was said with a touch of distain by Jesus.

George ignored him. "You will start with the one on your left. This is our premium regular margarita. Tequila, Cointreau and lime juice. Salt and a slice of lime on the rim."

Chris was the first to say, "I like it!"

"So this is what we get, either frozen or on the rocks, when we just say we want a margarita?"

"This is the top shelf margarita. The difference from the house drink is the brand of tequila, and we use Cointreau instead of a mix."

"Good." "Yes, great." "Can we have seconds?" "I must add this to the afternoon snack menu."

Annie closed her eyes as she savored the flavor. This was one of her favorite drinks.

"Next, the second one from the left, is the grapefruit ginger margarita. This isn't as sweet as the regular. It's a little tart. It's got white tequila, ginger liqueur, Grand Marnier and grapefruit juice. Garnished, of course, with salt and lime."

Once again, Annie closed her eyes. This was wonderful. Smooth. The combined taste of ginger and grapefruit was refreshing. Now this was her favorite.

George gave everyone time to taste and comment, then went on. "Number three. This is the Moscow Mule. White tequila, ginger beer and lime. Salt on the rim and a slice of lime to garnish."

Annie was running out of favorites.

"There are three to go. We're getting a little more exotic now. The next one is the blood orange margarita. Silver tequila, freshly squeezed blood oranges, lime juice, and Cointreau, garnished with a blood orange wheel and salt. Isn't this pretty?"

"It tastes better if I sip from a different part of the glass every time. Why is that?"

"The secret is how you do the rim. For this drink, you slide the blood orange slice all the way around the rim, dip the glass in salt, and put the slice on the edge. If you garnish with lime, you do the same."

They moved on to the next to the last drink.

"This is the elderflower margarita. Smooth and sweet. For this, we use silver tequila again, and add lime juice, elderflower liqueur, and of course it's garnished with lime and salt. This has what I call a bright citrus flavor."

Annie lost track of her favorite drink. She looked at the last one, counting to herself to make herself wait until George announced it. It seemed to take forever, but finally, he gave permission.

"Last one. This is the mole margarita, a dessert drink. Tequila, lime juice, mole sauce – that's chocolate, Annie – agave nectar, Cointreau. It's rimmed with Mexican chocolate and a little chili powder."

"I knew it was chocolate, George."

"Just making sure. Which one is your favorite?"

"All of them. Each one was. As soon as I tasted it. This is the last one, so it's my current favorite."

"Do we have to come in to work tomorrow, Annie?"

"What's tomorrow? Sunday? If it's Sunday, no."

"Tomorrow is Wednesday."

"Then yes. You have to come in tomorrow. And tomorrow night, you have to go to Sassy P's and paint a pumpkin."

"Right."

As the group got up to leave the table, Annie saw Frank enter the Tap. He looked around, then walked with a purposeful stride to the booth where Dennis still sat.

Frank didn't notice Annie – or any of his friends – as he walked toward the table. He had one reason to be here. He was going to take care of business and go home.

He didn't even ask permission to sit down. He sat and waved the server away before she got to the table.

Dennis looked at him, eyes bleary from two too many beers. "Whadaya want?"

"I want you to leave this town and never come back. What will it take to make you do that?"

"I told Mem. I need fifty thousand."

"That's ridiculous. What will it take, and make it reasonable."

"Fifty thousand, or I'm a dead man. One thousand won't do it, five thousand won't do it. Even ten thousand would just make them laugh. I need fifty thousand."

"Where do you think Mem is going to come up with that kind of money?"

"She's got a business, savings, Diana works, I'll bet she has money put back. She's just like her mother. I'll bet that boyfriend of hers can come up with something."

"Ha. Have you seen that beater he drives?"

"Yeah. It's that one right there, isn't it?" Dennis pointed out the window to a rusty pickup truck parked on The Avenue.

"That's it. And Diana doesn't even own a car. Mem's car is ten years old and held together with duct tape and baling twine. Where do you think they've got money stashed?"

"She owns part of that building. I looked it up."

"So you think someone is going to, what? Loan her the money? Buy the business from her in twenty-four hours?"

"She's got rich friends. All around town. She knows everybody. I know she can get it."

"Why would she?"

"Because she still loves me, that's why."

Frank huffed.

"She does. Deep down, she does."

"But for some reason, she continues to say no."

"She hasn't kicked me out yet. I'll wear her down."

"Let me tell you something, buster. I don't know why you need the money, but it can't be for any legal reason. If you don't leave town, and leave tomorrow morning, I'm going to file a complaint and get a restraining order. It will all come out in court. You aren't going to wear her down. If you come near her again, you'll pay the price."

Frank pushed up from the table and stomped out the door.

It was late by the time Billy got to the marina. Once again, he heard voices outside Mr. Cooper's place. He finally remembered the name of that man. Dennis.

Billy didn't bother stopping to listen tonight. Dennis was talking loud enough that he could hear without difficulty. Billy got past the junk boat, and there they were. A dim light over the door of Mr. Cooper's dilapidated house trailer illuminated the two men.

Dennis paced up and down. His arms waved in a wide arc. His face was red, his voice was loud. He's drunk, thought Billy. He was saying something about Mem, and Frank, and…was that Diana? That nobody had any money. Nobody! But he had to get it. Somehow he had to get it.

By now, Billy was past them, but the conversation had become interesting. When he reached the next broken down boat, he stopped and crouched behind it, continuing to listen.

"He'll be sending guys soon. Real soon. I gotta have a plan."

Mr. Cooper's voice seemed soft in comparison. "You ain't gonna convince her. You gotta force her. Or force her friends. That's gotta be your plan."

Billy wanted to keep listening, but Porter entered the marina, singing a silly song at the top of his lungs. Billy turned and sprinted past the boat, so stupid old Porter wouldn't give him away for snooping.

He got to the cabin before the rest of the crew, got a beer and sat down to wait.

When they all arrived, Billy asked, "Did the pigs come talk to you?"

He got nods all around the room.

"What'd ya say, Justin?"

Justin looked at his feet. "I told 'em I been workin' on a project in the garage every night for a month. Showed 'em what my dad's been doin'."

"Your dad gonna back you up?"

"I dunno. Fer sure the old lady won't."

Billy thought about that for a minute. Justin's family had money. His parents didn't have jobs; they had careers. His brother graduated from college with a degree in engineering, and a sister was in medical school.

Billy huffed, then looked at Marc. Marc looked up at the hole in the hull of the boat. "Told 'em I couldn't remember. The old lady just cried. She didn't say nothin'. Just shook her head and cried. She said I was hard to handle 'cause I got no dad."

"And they said okay? That you couldn't remember?"

"I'm here, ain't I?"

"What about you, Dallas?"

"I tole 'em I go ta bed ever' night by ten, and if somethin' was to have happened after ten, weren't me. They looked at my old man, but he was dead drunk and it weren't even noon. They got nothin'."

Porter was prepared with an answer. "They asked me where I was, and I told them I was in my room watching TV. They asked what I watched, and I told them everything that came on for each night we did stuff."

"You just offered it up? On the fifth I watched this, and on the twelfth I watched that?"

"Yeah."

"Didn't they ask how you knew the dates?"

Porter looked at his feet. "Well, yeah, they kinda wanted to know that, but I said, you know, you're askin' about that stuff been happenin', and I just remember the dates is all."

Billy grabbed another beer, opened it, took a long drink and looked around at his crew. His crew. The idiots of all time.

"You guys. What dunderbutts. Well, you better have a good alibi for the next one. We're gonna have fun."

Porter looked at Billy with a goofy smile, then around the room, head bobbing to some beat. Three faces looked down at the floor of the stinking, rotting boat.

Justin got home a little after midnight. His mother was in the kitchen, as she always was until he got home. She looked at him, said nothing, picked up her cup of tea and went to the bedroom.

Justin stood, leaning against the counter. He put his head into his hands and cried.

9

On Wednesday morning, Annie almost stepped on two paper butterflies at the bottom of the steps. Several others littered the floor between the steps and the kitchen.

She found Henrie multi-tasking. He read the morning paper with one eye and watched the news with another.

Roving reporter Dan Tapper could be seen in front of Babar Foods. His mouth was moving; Annie could hear nothing.

"Why did you mute it, Henrie?"

In reply, Henrie punched the remote. Annie could hear, "…and this terrorist attack against a Muslim woman will not go unanswered."

"Terrorist attack? Muslim woman?"

Henrie punched the remote again. "Now you see why it was muted. Juanita's article in the morning newspaper has the correct version of events, but Mr. Tapper's incendiary remarks will be the ones that will be remembered."

"Is he out there now?"

"I believe this was filmed yesterday around noon."

"Thank goodness he didn't come into the Café. I would have decked him."

"And that is probably why he did not go into the Café."

Henrie tossed the newspaper to the table and rose to pour a cup of coffee for himself. "When I stepped out to pick up the paper, I saw Ginger and James coming from the beach or park, I am not certain which, carrying what looked to be sleeping bags. What do you think they were doing?"

"I'll bet they were watching for the bullies. Jolly said something about it, that she was concerned the kids might do something stupid. Like that."

"They must be careful. They are no match for that group of ruffians."

"I'll say something to Pete. Better him than Laila. She's probably angry enough about the news. I'd better stop in this morning. Hey, what did you think of those margaritas last night?"

"I believe I will lay in some private stock for my evening enjoyment."

"Henrie, you slay me."

Annie grew quiet. She stared at the kitchen table. Henrie followed her look.

Tiger Lily lay flat on the table, covering part of the newspaper, but not all, and her paw moved slowly across the words of the lead story. Sassy Pants and Mr. Bean sat quietly on either side, leaning in to watch her paw as it moved.

Annie and Henrie watched until Tiger Lily got to the end of the story. She sat up, still looking at the paper, while the little ones seemed to look at her expectantly.

"Did you understand it, Lily Girl?"

Three cats looked up quickly and jumped to the floor. They ran from the room.

Annie and Henrie looked at one another for a long moment.

"Do you think…"

"Is it possible…"

"Should I worry…"

"Tell me, what would you worry about first?"

"You're right. Best leave it alone."

"I am going to leave that newspaper right there for the time being. I must get ready for our guests."

"Oh. Yes. Guests. Who's coming today?"

"A group of women that call themselves the Palindrome Gals."

"Them! They sound like fun."

"Yes, they do, and they will be here through Sunday, as they are vendors for the OktoberFest."

"Which ones do what, again?"

"Hannah is a face painter. She will be in the back room. Anna and Eve sell jewelry from Nepal. Nan and Emme have a bookstore; both are authors but they sell other books as well. I understand they concentrate on what they call cozy mysteries, whatever that might be, and romance novels."

"And they're all friends?"

"They registered via a group telephone call. I could barely get a word in amidst all the laughter."

"It will be good to have a house filled with fun. For once."

Annie called to her cats and announced it was time to leave. On the sidewalk, as the cats turned to go to work, she said, "I'll stop in and see you later, kids. I have things to do on the other side of The Avenue."

Tiger Lily did an about face. She would learn more if she went with Annie than if she went to the Café.

Annie went first to DoubleGood. Holly was at the counter. She offered Annie a chair, kept there so anyone wanting to have a conversation could do it at eye level. Holly lived in a wheelchair.

Annie sat. Tiger Lily jumped into Holly's lap. "Is it set up? Ready to go?"

"Yes. We just have to decide where you want it. I reviewed the tapes from last night. For the most part, it was pretty boring, but I could tell you who left Mo's Tap with Geraldine, if ya know what I'm talkin' about."

Annie laughed. "I'm going to have to be good about this, not look at it unless something is wrong. Except, you know, I'll have to take a look every now and then, just to make sure the cameras are working. Are there long, boring parts? Where nothing happens?"

"They are motion activated. Look. I have all the cameras set on the screen; each one in a square. They're labeled at the bottom, so you know which one is recording. Let's scroll them all back to midnight."

Holly did what she needed to do, and the screens came into focus.

"Look. They're all blank, and then this one comes active."

Annie and Tiger Lily watched as Geraldine left the bar with... "No! Are she and Everett separated again?"

"I don't think so."

Then the camera that had gone live went black as another camera picked them up. On it went, until Geraldine and her "friend" got into her car and drove away. Tiger Lily pawed at the monitor.

"That settles it. This is going to be my morning wake-up."

"Annie!"

"All right, all right. I'll be good. I'll just do a quick check every morning to make sure they're still working. Do you think we should make an announcement? Let people know these are up?"

"No. That would defeat the purpose. Businesses put cameras outside all the time. They're a great tool for the police when something goes wrong. This is the price we pay."

"You're right. I'll just have to be sure that I remember not to do something embarrassing, like fix a wedgie or pick my nose."

"Good thinking at all times. You never know who might be watching. So. You decided on the kitchen. Are you sure that's where you want to set it up?"

"Henrie and I measured the cabinet above the computer in the kitchen. It needs to be somewhere we can both keep an eye on it, but where it is not seen by our guests. If we put it there, we aren't losing that much storage space, and we can close the cupboard door to cover it.

Tiger Lily gave a soft purr and tapped Annie's knee. She agreed.

Annie continued "We would have to take out at least one shelf, and maybe do something with that middle piece. I have the measurements." Annie copied the text to herself and sent it to Holly.

"Henrie will watch it so he knows what's going on. He won't tell town secrets. Unless we need to know. Like this.

About Geraldine. I'm going to have a hard time keeping quiet."

"It's probably all over town already, anyway. People at Mo's saw it, certainly, and this may not have been the first time."

"Hmmmm. So what do I need to know about this system?"

"It's a thermal imaging system. It detects the heat of objects, so it doesn't need light. If people – like the bully boys – wear dark colors at night, you'll still be able to see them. This is good for long-range, so they'll be able to detect people on the median also. And it works twenty-four hours a day."

"Sounds like just what we need." Annie pulled her cellphone out of her pocket. "I'm going to call Boone to see if he can install this in our cupboard."

"Good idea. Send him over here first, so he can see and measure the unit. Then I can pack it up and he can take it with him."

"Thanks, Holly."

Annie walked out, phone to her ear and cat at her heels. She had talked to both Boone and Henrie before stepping into Babar Foods.

Laila was behind the deli counter, filling one of her Pakistani salad dishes. Tiger Lily went behind the counter and stood up, patting Laila's thigh.

In a dramatic voice, Annie said, "I hear there's a Muslim woman in town who just got terrorized."

"If it were anyone but you, Annie…" Laila reached for a homemade cat treat and gave it to Tiger Lily.

"I'm sorry. I couldn't help it. Did you complain to the television station?"

"Last night, after I saw it the first time. They didn't change it, though. The same story ran this morning."

"That's the one I saw. Poor misunderstood Dan. Unfortunately, he's a joke to us but the Word of God to others. People believe that crap! Maybe I'll write a letter to the editor. The paper is always feuding with WQVX. Maybe they'll put it on the front page. Hey. I have a better idea."

Annie's cellphone came out again, and she looked in her contacts to find a number. She dialed, and after two rings, she got an answer.

"Juanita, this is Annie Mack. Hey, I have a story for you. You got the vandalism right, but we need to do something about WQVX and their misinformed reporting. Are you interested? ... Great. Come on over to Babar Foods and talk to Laila. She can set the public straight about a thing or two."

Annie hung up. "Go for it, Laila. Don't hold back."

"Thanks, Annie. I'll let you know how it goes."

Annie left, cat still at her heels. She stopped at CyberHealth next. She approached Mem at the counter. "Do you have time to join me for a cup of tea?"

"I do."

"Pick the flavor. It looks like Tiger Lily already chose a table by the window."

Annie had just taken a chair next to Tiger Lily when Harrison Jones approached from behind.

"Hey, Annie. I was in the back checking my email and I heard you talking to Mem. I just wanted to say hello. And, wow, what a time to come. Vandals in Chelsea. Who woulda thought."

Tiger Lily jumped from the chair to the tabletop, the better to receive a pet from Harrison. He obliged.

"Harrison, it's good to see you. Do you want to join us for tea?"

"No, I'll let you women talk. Just wanted to say hello. I think I'll be seeing you again tonight. Diana and I are going to paint a couple of pumpkins."

"Great. I'm really glad, Harrison, that you and Diana are together. This has been great for her."

"Good to know. She's good for me, too. Well, here's Mem. I'll see you later."

Harrison rose as Mem set down the tea service tray. Tiger Lily had to jump back to a chair to make room for the china teapot with a funky cosy – this one was a ladybug design – and mismatched china cups and saucers. "We're having South African Honeybush tea. A serious red tea for a serious conversation. Good morning, Tiger Lily. I brought part of a cream cheese scone for you."

Annie watched as Tiger Lily laid into the scone. "You're going to put on five pounds today." Then to Mem, she said, "How did you know it would be serious?"

"I talked to Frank. He told me you were concerned."

"So tell me. What's up? I know your ex is in town. I saw him at Mo's Tap last night."

"Yes, he's in town. He's been at one of the heated cabins at the state campground for a few days. He blew in, ambushed Diana one afternoon when she got home from work, and proceeded to try to worm his way back into our lives. Diana is livid that I'm actually talking to him."

"I thought Diana was angry that you divorced him."

"She grew out of that. As an adult, she looked back and saw what I saw, and as an adult, there was no way she could blame me that he divorced her as well."

"Absent fathers should beware of daughters scorned. Why is he trying to get back into your life?"

"He wants money. He always wanted money. That's why I finally divorced him. One scheme after another. He'd go to work at an orchard for a while, meet some ne'er do well, hear about a get rich quick scheme, quit that job, lose a bundle, go to work for a farmer, meet another ne'er do well…. It was an endless cycle. Every penny I made – more than that, even – he spent. It took me years to get out of debt when I finally divorced him."

"I didn't know. You overcame a lot."

"I did. And now I have a business, I own this part of the building, I have some savings, some hope of a comfortable retirement, and he wants back in."

"And Diana is angry that you're talking to him."

"Yes. She thinks I'll succumb."

"Really? She thinks that of you?"

"Well, she can't understand why I don't just tell him to hit the road."

Annie let that sink in for a while. Finally, she asked, "Why don't you just tell him to hit the road?"

Mem looked at Annie, then looked back at her cup of tea. "He's really in trouble this time. I have a hard time turning my back on the man who gave me Diana."

"What kind of trouble is it?"

"He says he owes money to a man he calls a gangster. The gangster said if he doesn't come up with a lot of money quickly, he'll regret it, and so will everyone else in his life."

"So he ran here to re-involve you in his life so you could possibly be hurt as well?"

Mem looked up at Annie quickly. "You're right, Annie. I didn't see it that way. But you're right. Now Diana and I might become targets as well. How could I be so blind?"

"He gave you Diana. And frankly, do you know if he really is in trouble with...the mob, I guess?"

"He didn't offer any proof, but what proof would he have? You've given me something to think about, that's for sure."

"What does Frank think about all of this?"

"He's trying to stay out of it."

"He is?"

"Yes. He told me this was something that I had to work through, and he wouldn't try to encourage me one way or another."

"Really. Hmmm."

"What, Annie? What do you know, or think that you know?"

"I'm sorry, Mem. I put myself in the middle and I shouldn't have. But you're one of my best friends, so...I saw Frank last night, too. As I was leaving Mo's. He came in and sat down with Dennis. I don't know how long they talked. I left."

Annie thought about the camera system. She could – if she really wanted to – go back to see how long Frank stayed. If she really wanted to. She would have to ask Holly how long the film was active, or when it started to tape over.

Annie left the tea shop, Tiger Lily at her heels, feeling both sad and angry. Sad that she had given Mem information about Frank, and angry that Frank had done something to qualify as tattle material. She had to console herself with the fact that Mem would tell her about Chris, if there was something she needed to know.

Annie's next stop was the police department. She needed to talk to Pete about her camera system. Tiger Lily curled into Cyril's side while Pete and Annie talked.

"Hey, Annie. I was just going over to the Café for some coffee, and here you are."

"Let's talk for a minute, then I'll take you over and buy you a cup."

"Good deal for me. What's up?"

"You know I put cameras in. They went live yesterday."

"I'm glad you did. How long is the tape good?"

"I thought about that just a few minutes ago. I didn't ask. Now's as good a time as any."

Annie's cellphone came out again, and she dialed DoubleGood. Holly answered. "Hey, Annie. What now?"

"How long will the tape be good?"

"You have two hard drives, a main and a back-up. Both are a terabyte."

"What does that mean?"

"It will be out there for a long, long time. Months. It will depend on how much activity there is in the evening. You can count on almost continual taping during the day, but it slows down when no one is on the screen. Since you're covering all of The Avenue, it won't slow down a lot, but some."

"And it will all be date and time stamped?"

"Yes. By the way, Boone just left with it. He's on his way to the Inn."

"Great. Thanks, Holly." Annie closed the call and said to Pete, "Months. She says months."

"Great. Surely, if something happens, we won't need that kind of time. So tell me, Annie, are you going to start watching the night streets and telling all our secrets?"

"I could, but…no. I saw something from last night, but I'm not telling."

"Oh, come on. What was it?"

"Geraldine and…I'm not saying who."

"That's old news, Annie. They've been meeting at Mo's for a couple of weeks now."

"Why hasn't George told me? Or Candice?"

"They're great bartenders. What happens at Mo's stays at Mo's, and everyone in town knows it."

"But you know…"

"Because I've been at Mo's. I haven't told you either, have I. Come on. Say it with me. What. Happens At. Mo's. Stays. At. Mo's."

Annie said it with him. And she thought about her faux pas. She told Mem about something that happened at Mo's. And she would probably do it again.

Annie almost forgot to relay Henrie's conversation about Ginger. When she did, she was once again sad to relay bad news.

Pete didn't take it well. After banging his fist on the desk and saying a few words that best go unrepeated, he said, "That girl is in trouble. She told me they were studying for mid-terms. She knows how dangerous those boys are."

After Pete wound down, they walked to the Café. Annie treated Pete to a Mexican latte. Tiger Lily escorted Cyril behind the coffee counter where Trudie slipped both of them a treat.

10

Five women entered the Inn with a burst of laughter. Henrie materialized in the foyer, and two large cats appeared out of thin air like bookends on either side of him.

"Welcome to the KaliKo Inn. I am Henrie. To my left and right are your hostesses, Kali and Ko."

"They're ADORABLE!" shrieked one woman.

"Will they COME to me?" shrieked another.

Kali and Ko moved as one to hide behind Henrie's legs.

"They will get to know you on their own terms. Please, come in, have a seat. May I serve coffee? Tea?"

As the women exclaimed over the cats, the ambiance, the fresh flowers, the pastel colors that changed from room to room, and the coffee that Henrie served, he thought to himself, this is worse than having a house full of young children. But his smile remained in place.

The roar calmed to something a little more dull, and eventually, all of them seated with coffee, the first woman to have shrieked introduced herself. "I'm HANNAH. I do the FACE PAINTS. And THIS," she pointed around the room at each woman as she named them, "is ANNA, and EVE – they sell JEWELRY from NEPAL. You'll LOVE it. And NAN – she writes COZY mysteries – and EMME – she writes ROMANCE novels."

"Please tell me what a cozy mystery might be."

Laughter all around, but Nan eventually rose from the laugh to answer. "They're REAL EASY to read, and they're FUNNY, and they have an amateur DETECTIVE."

"Or TWO," added Emme.

"Or MORE, but they're EASY. You know, MURDER without GORE, ROMANCE without SEX, NOTHING that will slow down your READING. You can BREEZE RIGHT THROUGH them. They're GREAT vacation books."

"I may know a few amateur detectives. I should introduce you before you leave town."

Laughter again. "Please DO! I'd LOVE to meet them!"

Henrie held it together long enough to give them the standard tour and to show them to their rooms. Three women had separate rooms; Nan and Emme were in the same room, even though they had asked for five rooms.

Hannah – with a room for herself – said, "We heard this was a GREAT town to meet MEN, so we wanted to be PREPARED. You know, in case we actually MEET MEN! GET it?"

Emme added, "Are you SURE there isn't another ROOM? I don't mind SHARING with NAN, but if we all get LUCKY, we'll be out of SPACE."

"I could allow you a separate room tonight, but tomorrow, alas, that room will be taken. Perhaps a cabana on the beach would be of use."

"Oh, HENRIE, YOU'RE a HOOT!"

Henrie retreated, hoots intact. Kali and Ko had long since hidden in the library. Henrie looked around the corner. Sure enough, he saw two dilute calico tails poking out from under the television table. Of course, they thought they were well hidden.

A few minutes later, Henrie heard voices in the foyer.

"Lets go to the CAFÉ for lunch!" "NO! The WINERY!" "We'll be at the WINERY TONIGHT, you know, to PAINT PUMPKINS." "So OKAY, the CAFÉ it IS!"

Annie was leaving the Café, having helped during the lunch rush, but she stopped to give Tiger Lily a hug. As she stood there, she looked out the window, down the sidewalk toward the Inn.

Five women appeared to revel in the crisp fall air. They pointed and exclaimed to one another about the sights, stopping to gape at the mess across the street. The insurance company would "investigate" before approving painting and repair, so the building would wear its angry slashes of color for a while.

When the women reached the Café, Annie opened the door and stood aside for them to enter.

"You must be the Palindrome Gals. I'm Annie."

"HELLO!"

"What HAPPENED over there?"

"We've never seen ANYTHING like THAT!"

"We've had some vandalism in town. It's very unusual, and probably related to Halloween, but the police are on it. They expect to make some arrests soon."

"How AWFUL!"

Annie smiled, but cringed inwardly. Henrie must have had a mild heart attack while showing these women around.

"Did you get settled at the Inn?"

"YES! It's BEAUTIFUL!"

"I have the BEST VIEW! It's the LAKE!"

"But I have the BEST ROOM! I can see EVERYTHING that HAPPENS on The AVENUE!"

Annie smiled and walked, holding her arms in welcome as she showed the women to a large table next to the window. "You can look at The Avenue from here, too. Sadie will be your server. Enjoy your lunch, and I'm sure I'll see you later."

Annie walked back to the hostess stand. Tiger Lily sat, transfixed, watching as the women sat and exclaimed over the menu, the décor, the funky tables and colorful chairs.

"You can stay right here, darlin'. You don't have to go to their table. I'm sure they can make their own decisions."

Tiger Lily looked at Annie and blinked once. She jumped down and followed Annie out the door.

Annie looked down. A cat followed her. "Tiger Lily, I have errands to run this afternoon. Why don't you go on home?"

Tiger Lily blinked once and walked toward the Inn, leaving Annie to take care of business.

Annie crossed The Avenue and went to Bloomin' Crazy. Clara and Valeria worked on several fresh flower bouquets, each one in a different color scheme.

Annie said, "Clara, are these mine?"

"Yes they are. I asked you to stop in so I could explain."

"Explain what?"

"You expect these on Thursday, but tomorrow I have to get over to the community building and help my Women Empowered group put up a CanStruction thing."

"That's not a problem. What kind of can thing are you going to make?"

"My group is making three figures: a girl playing basketball, an older girl – or a young woman – in a chemistry lab, and a woman shattering a glass ceiling."

"I can't wait to see it!" Frankly, Annie still had trouble imagining what a CanStruction project would or could resemble. She should Google it, she thought.

Annie watched as Clara put fall touches into two arrangements. Crystal vases – one oversized and one medium sized – were filled with a variety of blue flowers. They would go to the Inn. The arrangements were elegant; Annie thought the oriental cattails added a nice touch.

Valeria bent over two arrangements, one with red flowers and one with green. The red arrangement – headed for the Winery – was in a red lacquered gourd box, the green one in a pale green version of a pumpkin. Both were low arrangements and received dwarf cattails.

Valeria hadn't finished the pumpkin vase going to the yoga studio or the yellow squash vase going to Mo's. Cattails and silk autumn-colored leaves lay beside them.

Annie walked back over to Clara, who now worked on a crystal vase filled with purple blossoms. "I'm putting orange, red and yellow silk fall leaves in these. Adding a little color. And look what Valeria found for Bon Vivant."

Clara reached over to pick up a photograph and handed it to Annie. Her fine dining restaurant opened on Friday and Saturday night at the Café. The purple flowers went to the coffee bar, and a more colorful arrangement took its place on the hostess stand.

Annie saw multi-colored flowers and silk birds in a white gourd vase with a fall scene painted all around it.

"Beautiful."

As Annie got up to leave, Valeria said, "There, Clara. That one. He's been following me. Well, they all have, but it's the one in the middle that keeps talking to me.

Clara and Annie looked out the window.

"Which ones are they, Annie?"

"Those are the ones I call the three musketeers. Dallas, Justin and Marc."

The three women continued to stare out the window while they talked.

"Why do you call them that?"

"The leader is Billy, and the hanger-on is Porter. It was his dad that mugged me."

"Oh, right."

Valeria looked over at the two women but kept her mouth shut.

Annie continued. "So these three are the musketeers. All for one and one for all. They can be better than Billy, but I think they can also be worse. Depends on what they want, I guess, and how desperate they are. The one in the middle is Justin."

"Justin. Okay. So, should I be afraid?"

"Yes," said two women at once.

"Have you said anything to Pete?" asked Annie.

"No. I didn't think they'd done anything bad enough."

"What kind of things does he say?"

"Nothing sinister. Things like, hi, how do you like living here, things like that."

"That's not sinister, but it could lead to something worse. Let Pete know, get it on record, and let him be the judge. He can also give you advice."

Annie waited until the young men left The Avenue, then she stepped out to do a little grocery shopping.

Two rough-looking men walked into Mo's and slipped into a table in front of the window. They could both see across the street, but only one, Bernie, could watch CyberHealth without turning.

Sam faced the other direction. He watched as Annie left the flower shop. "She's one of those friends. She owns everything on this side. She'll have dough."

Bernie turned. "Which one?"

"Straight grayish hair, going into the grocery store now."

"Okay. We can think about her."

"Ya know, all these stores are owned by women. They all got dough, some pro'bly more than others. Take that flower shop lady."

They both turned to look at Bloomin' Crazy. Clara stepped out, pulling a wagon loaded with fresh flower arrangements.

"See? Lotsa orders. Lotsa dough."

"But people don't keep dough like they used to. It's all this cloud stuff now. Debit cards, credit cards."

"But they got it in the bank. We can figure out how to squeeze somethin', but we're gonna have to get to that ex-wife. They'll pay for her. They won't pay for him."

"So, tonight?"

"Yeah. Tonight. I heard people talkin' about this thing going on at the Winery tonight. We'll sit right here and watch for that boyfriend of hers – Frank? – to come get her. Before he gets outa there, we'll go in."

"What if he goes in the back way? There's gotta be a back way into the apartment."

"You're right. Someone has ta sit over there and watch. That would be you."

"Why me?"

"Cause I got seniority."

"Seniority? You talk like we work at a bank or somethin'."

"We do. It's the 'or somethin'."

"Where'm I gonna sit?"

"I don't know. Sit on yer hands fer all I care, but after we have a burger, that's what yer gonna do."

11

Tiger Lily waited in the foyer for everyone else to come home. She had arrived way too early for snacks.

While she sat on a couch, cleaning her paws, a strange cat poked his head into the cat door. It was a tentative poke.

Tiger Lily stopped cleaning her paw, but it remained in mid-air. *"Who are you?"*

"Um, I'm Daryll?"

"Daryll? What are you doing here?"

"Um, I heard there were detective cats here?"

Daryll was a multi-colored cat, looking somewhat like Sassy Pants. His tabby markings framed the white fur that started at his forehead and ended at his toes. He had a face that said "what's going on here" and a tabby spot under his lower lip that accentuated a perpetual look of confusion.

"Yes. I'm a detective. My name is Tiger Lily. Can I help you?"

Daryll walked into the foyer slowly, looking left and right as he did so. Eventually, he reached the sofa and sat, looking up at Tiger Lily.

"Um, I'm Daryll?"

"Yes. You said that. Why do you need a detective?"

"Um, there's some men? Some mean men? They came to the state park last night?"

"You live at the state park?"

"Um, yes? I stay with the manager? He has a cabin at the campground?"

"*Who are these men?*"

"*I don't know? They sat and waited for this one man to get to his cabin last night? And when he got home? They had a real loud fight?*"

Tiger Lily noticed the way all of Daryll's statements were phrased as questions. She figured the little cat was just nervous. She asked, "*You want to protect the man?*"

"*Um, no? I'm scared they might do something to my human? He went out and told them to leave? They weren't very nice to him?*"

"*I don't know what we can do, Daryll. Let's talk about it and try to figure something out. Come on into my office.*"

Tiger Lily jumped off the couch and led the tentative Daryll to the dining room and into the detective agency. Tiger Lily took a cushion and motioned that he should do the same. Daryll touched a pillow, pushed it a few times with his right front paw, then climbed up gingerly, almost as if he expected the pillow would bite. Tiger Lily allowed him to take his time.

When he seemed to be comfortable, she said, "*Tell me about the man, first. Who is he?*"

"*I think his name is Dennis? He seems to know the town? He walks up the street and talks to a woman? I think he calls her Mem?*"

"*That would be Mem's ex-husband. I heard about him.*"

Daryll seemed impressed. "*Wow. You're good.*"

"*No, I just get around. Tell me what you know about him.*"

110

"*Um, I don't know much? Because he doesn't have any other visitors? He told those men about Mem? He said she had money? She could pay?*"

"*No!*"

"*Yes? And they asked how soon he'd have the money? And he said he was working on it? But there was a problem? Some guy named Frank?*"

"*No!*"

"*Yes? And they got real mean? They said he was out of time? And that's when my human went outside? He told them to leave?*"

"*What happened then?*"

"*Those men? They said really mean things to my human? And they told him to mind his own business? And my human came back and locked the door?*"

"*This sounds bad. This sounds very bad.*"

Tiger Lily heard noises in the foyer and heard two loud thumps from the library. The other cats were coming.

"*Now don't be scared. There will be lots of cats here pretty soon.*"

"*Um, I know two cats? They got dumped at the park in the winter? Now they live on this street?*"

"*That would be Fat Cat and Scaredy Cat. Excuse me. Their humans gave them other names.*"

"*They told me? They said they have real names now? Simon Finnegan and Oscar McMurphy? They told me to come here?*"

"*That's how you knew to come. That explains it. Well, here are the rest of them.*"

Cats poked their heads under the tablecloth and started at the sight of the new cat. As they entered, one by one, they said, *"Who are you?" "Trill!" "You're in my seat!" "We gots a new cat?" "Where'd you come from?"*

Tiger Lily shushed them one at a time and finally got their attention. *"This is Daryll. He lives at the state park, and he's come to see about getting some help for his human. Fat Cat and Scaredy Cat told him about us."*

"What's wrong with his human?" "We're ready to help!" "Trill!" "Hey, Daryll. Ize Sassy Pants."

Henrie lifted the corner of the tablecloth to set down seven bowls of treats. He noticed the new cat and said, very politely, "How do you do? I'm Henrie. Wait here and I will get another bowl."

Henrie returned shortly with another bowl of treats. He set the bowl in front of Daryll. "I hope you enjoy it."

As Henrie left, he thought to himself, how often is this going to happen? Are we going to feed every stray in town?

Daryll looked around. Everyone was eating, so he did the same. Soon, he had finished his bowl and looked up to see all the other cats looking at him. *"Did I do something wrong?"*

"No, Daryll, we were just waiting for you to finish. Before you tell your story again, I have to tell everyone what I learned today."

Tiger Lily told the assembled group what she learned about the camera system, where the monitor could be found, about Pete's interest in the camera system, and about Laila and the reporter coming to interview her.

"Maybe Mommy will turn on the news tonight, and we have to read the paper tomorrow. Now this is important. Mommy talked to Mem this morning, and what Daryll is going to tell us has to do with this."

Tiger Lily told them everything she had learned about Dennis from Mem. Then she turned to Daryll.

"Now tell them what you told me."

Daryll repeated his story, still tentative, still phrasing his sentences as questions. But he got through it, from beginning to end, looking around at cat faces as he did so.

When he finished, no one made a sound. Then a rush of questions and statements came out.

"Wot we gonna do?" "Trill!" "We have to tell Mem!" "We have to tell Frank!" "Can we tell Mommy?" "When are we going to see Cyril?" "We have to tell Pete!" "Tiger Lily, are you going to write it down?"

Daryll stared from one to the other. He was so impressed. They seemed to have it all together. He had done the right thing by coming here.

12

The Winery was the place to be on Wednesday night. Annie and Henrie entered an already full back room, but seats had been saved for them. They made their way toward a table in the middle of the room.

Annie waved at Chris. He was behind the bar with Jet, coordinating painting materials and supervising the choosing of pumpkins. Cheryl and Janet had already chosen pumpkins for Annie and Henrie.

"I don't know if I'm going to paint one."

"Sure, you're going to paint one. It might look funny, but that's how we'll know it's yours."

Annie turned as she heard, from the back of the room, "I want one of THOSE!" "What a HANDSOME GUY!"

She couldn't tell who they were talking about, but hoped it wasn't Chris.

Minnie appeared with another server and a couple of trays loaded with wine flights. "I figured you wanted the flight, rather than a couple of glasses."

"Great. What are they?"

After Minnie placed flights in front of them, she handed a flyer to Annie. "Here's an explanation sheet. I'd go through it with you, but we're a little busy tonight."

"Thanks, Minnie." Annie looked at the sheet and read it aloud. "Okay. The first red wine is an 'Adobe Guadalupe, a mixture of Tempranillo, Grenache and Cabernet.' Mostly Tempranillo. Good with red meat, pasta, cheese and fish."

They tasted. Annie signed. "Good." She looked around the room, smiling and waving to anyone who looked back.

Diana gave a wave. She and Harrison sat at a four-top with two empty chairs.

"Let me do the next one." Cheryl grabbed the information sheet from Annie. "Baron Balche. Some kind of word Zinfandel. Oh. One of my favorites. Good with lamb and goat cheese. Do we have any lamb or goat cheese?"

Annie could hear Chris in the background. She chose to be a bad student and continued to talk to her tablemates, but she heard part of what he said.

"... ripe ... already checked to make sure there are no blemishes ... strong stem ..."

Annie took the wine information sheet back and read the next one. "This sounds good. 'Casa Madero. Shiraz Casa Grande.' This one is aged for at least two years, and we're supposed to taste cinnamon, hazelnut, chocolate and some kind of fruit."

Chris droned on. Well, he wasn't actually droning. Actually, his voice was strong and had a sexy lilt to it. But still, he was in the background. "... washed, and we sealed them ... when you take it home ... keep it out of direct sunlight ... bring it in if it rains or freezes ..."

Janet picked up the information sheet and read about the fourth wine, which some people had already started. "Okay. I can read this, but I'm going to hammer the pronunciation. Vee-nos Shee-mull Al-bar-roll-o, I've got this word, Nebbiolo. Dense, vanilla, plums, coffee and chocolate. It's supposed to taste woody."

"...each table has several brushes ... water ... notice tables covered in plastic ... soft pencils if you want to sketch ... have some stencils up here ...

Pete grabbed the information sheet. "You're too slow, guys. What's this next one. This is a Chardonnay from Casa Medero. We're supposed to eat this with peppers in walnut sauce. Do we have any of that? Or bananas flambe. That sounds good."

"...pictures up here of some examples ...

Annie finally looked at the front of the room. On a screen, photographs of painted pumpkins scrolled across, each one resting for several seconds while guests watched. She saw a picture of the Wolverine and another of Iron Man, someone must have painted himself, a group of pumpkins – a large one painted with the face of a man, a medium one with the face of a woman, and several smaller ones painted with the faces of children – animals, one that looked like an apple, and another like a pear.

Henrie took the information sheet for the last wine. "Allow me." Unlike everyone else, Henrie read this wine's information word for word. With perfect pronunciation. "'La Cetto. Sierra Blanca Sauvignon Blanc. Originating of a line of wines that features a new winemaking technique, which includes the innovative use of conical tanks. This is the first wine in Mexico to replace the traditional cork with an alternative top called Stelvin. This wine is excellent with fresh salads, seafood pasta and lobster.'"

Annie barely heard him, but she picked up the last glass and drank it down. "Look. Someone did the *Mona Lisa*. I can't do that." She saw night skies, outer space, patterns – stripes, polka dots, zig-zag lines. She saw Halloween themes, trees, leaf shapes.

"I can do leaves. I'll bet I can do leaves."

Then she saw the perfect pumpkin. Splotches, slashes and blobs. A piece of modern art on a pumpkin.

"That's what I'll do."

Pictures continued to scroll across the screen, but Annie grabbed a couple of brushes and went to work. "Let's paint some pumpkins."

Annie painted for a while, then she looked around. Chris and Jet circulated, stopping at each table. When Jet stopped at theirs, he exclaimed about the talent. He focused on Cheryl's start at the Hulk. Cheryl had a bit of artistic talent She used three shades of green, black, and red for the eyes.

He looked next at Janet's pumpkin. Janet had a bit of talent also. She had started to paint hers completely, showing the lake in brilliant sunset, a white sand beach on the bottom, dotted with shells and pebbles.

Annie said, "Jet, I don't see Mem and Frank. Didn't they pre-register?"

"They did, and they're the only ones that didn't come."

Annie looked back at the table. Diana was now there alone.

Her attention was captured when she heard from the back of the room, "YOU are so TALENTED!"

"FORGET that, Hannah. You mean he's so HANDSOME!"

"HEY, we're STAYING at the KALIKO INN. COME BACK with us. We'll have a PARTY."

"And BRING your cute FRIEND."

Annie didn't hear Chris's reply.

Pete tried to paint Cyril. Emphasis on the word "tried." Janet's only comment was, "Don't show him, Pete. He'll be insulted."

Ray was not about to be outdone by Pete. He painted Jock, and did a pretty good job of it.

Annie heard, "HELLO! WHO are YOU?" She turned in time to see Ian being dragged by the arm to the Palindrome table. Ian didn't look upset. He can handle himself, thought Annie.

Henrie showed off artistic talent that had somehow been unknown before. He started a scene with a man, just the bottom half, in an Adirondack chair, feet up on a small table. The arm of the chair showed the man's arm and hand cradling a glass of red wine. Around the chair were sands and tall grasses. Beyond his feet was white sand, a lake and a sunset with glorious clouds. Like Janet, he used the whole pumpkin.

Annie was speechless as she studied it.

She was distracted again with a, "Hey, HANDSOME, I think I need a STENCIL." One of the Palindrome Gals was at the front of the room. She was behind the tasting bar, and Chris was cornered, back to the wine racks, arms stretched as far to either side as they could get.

Annie stifled a smile, but laughed outright as Holly wheeled herself behind the bar. It looked like she asked Chris for help doing…Annie wasn't sure what, but the Palindrome Gal tweaked his cheek and left. Jet, from behind, leaned down to give Holly a kiss on her cheek. Chris did the same.

Annie's tablemates looked in wonder at Annie's masterpiece. The pumpkin had blobs, blotches and slashes of her signature colors, blue, red, green, yellow, orange and purple. At the bottom, she had painted her name in hard, straight slashes, making a geometric pattern of the letters.

"That's really good, Annie." "Really. Really good." "Who knew you had it in you?" "We will put this in the foyer next to the fresh flowers. It will accent the Inn perfectly."

At that moment, they heard sirens outside. Annie looked toward the door and motioned toward it with her head. Pete looked around. His second-in-command, Marco, stood in the doorway. When they made eye contact, Marco motioned for him to come. Pete jumped up, and Janet did, as well.

Annie looked at Diana's table. Diana was gone. Annie jumped up also and said to Henrie, "It's Mem. I know it's Mem."

Cyril and Jock were given full run of the Inn that evening. They ran through the house, knocked a few things down and chased cats through cat doors. When all the cats had gone places they couldn't follow, they went to the library and found paper butterflies to chew up and spit out.

Finally tired, they took a nap on the rug in the middle of the floor. The cats came, one by one, until a breathing, sighing pile made an even larger rug.

After a nap, Tiger Lily and Little Socks worked together to bring the dogs up to speed on the community. Cyril was able to share some things as well.

"Ginger is going to get herself in trouble. Pete thought she was staying over with James, studying for mid-terms, and Laila probably thought he was at our house. But they were in the park, watching for those bully boys. They think they're going to wreck the OktoberFest set-up. They've started to put things up, you know, and tomorrow, things will really be happening. They're going to set up games and food booths, and they already put all those cans in the community building."

"Did Ginger get grounded?"

"She convinced Pete they were really studying. She talked him into letting her go back to study with James tonight. She promised they would stay at the apartment, but I think they're going back to the park, and I don't think they're studying at all."

Little Socks said, *"The bully boys might try to scare them, but mostly, they're wrecking things. We have news about some bad men that might hurt Mem and Frank."*

Cyril and Jock sat up, knocking cats down in the process. Soon, everyone was sitting up and engaged in the conversation.

Cyril and Jock made plans to protect their friends. Tiger Lily promised to let Daryll, Fat Cat and Scaredy Cat know what was going on.

Mr. Bean said, *"I'll tell Tillie, too. She might be able to do something."*

They realized they were too late when Janet burst into the Inn. In a loud, scared voice, she called, "Cyril? Cyril, come on! Pete needs you!"

In three bounds, Cyril was in the foyer. He followed Janet outside on the run.

13

Thursday dawned clear and cold, perfect weather to set up for the Oktoberfest. Henrie had been up until the early hours of the morning, but nonetheless, he persisted.

He thought longingly about the hours when he could have slept. Instead, he spent them with Marco going over the video of The Avenue.

The search had been fruitless. Nothing useful was seen. Marco had said the men must have walked behind the building.

Henrie yawned, sighed, and went to work.

He prepared an egg casserole, French toast casserole, bacon, ham and sausage, toast and English muffins. In keeping with the Mexican theme of the month, he added sweet potato chorizo hash garnished with avocado, and a Tex-Mex version of chilaquiles, an entrée that needed more than one dish. One dish contained fried corn tortillas cooked in green chili salsa, sprinkled with grated longhorn cheese. A double dish to the side contained eggs over medium with lots of freshly ground black pepper in the front, and black beans spiced with cilantro in the back. For garnish, he added bowls of chopped red onion and dried ancho chilies.

Isabel had stopped in earlier with chipotle and jalapeno bagels and churro doughnuts from Mr. Bean's.

Henrie operated on automatic pilot. He could feel the lack of sleep. In a semi-daze he turned on the morning news, then went to the porch to pick up the paper.

On his way back in, he met five forceful women, charging down the stairs and up the back hallway at the same time. Almost as if they had set timers to leave their rooms simultaneously.

"OH, this smells HEAVENLY!"

"HERE are the CATS! LOOK at them! They're HIDING under that TABLE!"

"LOOK at this ADORABLE long-haired GRAY! Is he a BOY?"

Two of the women got on their knees and groped until they finally had Mo in their hands. Mo, generally a lover of all women, struggled to get free.

When he got free of one, another grabbed him. Then another.

"His FUR is so SOFT!"

"His FACE is so HANDSOME!"

Henrie threw the newspaper on the kitchen table, barely registering the two headlines that shared top billing as side-by-side articles. "WQVX Airs Fake News" and "Local Couple Kidnapped And Beaten."

He moved as quickly as he could toward Emme, who now held Mo. "Allow me."

Henrie took the struggling cat, who clung to his shoulder, shaken and frightened. He then told a brazen lie, for which he earned Mo's undying thanks. "Mo prefers to be left to himself."

He walked with Mo through the kitchen, opened his apartment door and placed him on the floor in the combination kitchen, dining and living room. Mo ran to Henrie's bedroom and hid under the bed.

Henrie turned and almost stepped on Mr. Bean, who had apparently been the next cat to be "loved" by the women. He joined Mo under the bed.

Henrie sighed and walked back to the dining room.

"HENRIE! This looks so GOOD!"

"SMELL that CHORIZO!"

"WHAT EXCITEMENT last night!"

"You were THERE, Henrie. What HAPPENED?"

"Were people HURT?"

"Do you KNOW them?"

"WHO is that DREAMBOAT that led the PUMPKIN painting? Do you KNOW him?"

"He's DREAMY."

"He's STEAMY!"

"Is he MARRIED?"

"I didn't see a RING."

"We INVITED him to come OVER last night, and to bring that CUTE GUY that HELPED him, but he SAID he had to go to WORK early."

"WHERE does he WORK, Henrie?"

Henrie would have replied to any of their questions, but the women kept talking, almost as if they didn't expect a response. He remained vigilant for a break in the conversation, ready to reply to what seemed to be the most salient point if a silence ever occurred. That didn't happen.

Annie came down, looking a little less refreshed than normal. Henrie smiled and nodded. Annie returned his gesture, turned to the table and said, "Good morning, ladies. Sleep well?"

"ANNIE! Good MORNING!"

"Who WAS it, Annie? WHO went AWAY in that AMBULANCE?"

Annie started to answer, but realized, like Henrie, that a response wasn't necessarily wanted. The jabber continued. In fact, Annie started reciting a poem in her head, one that seemed to define the situation. *Twas brillig, and the slithy toves did gyre and gimble in the wabe: all mimsy were the borogoves and the mome raths outgrabe.*

"ANNIE, do you know that DREAMBOAT?"

"SURE she does. She LIVES here!"

"Is he MARRIED? I've called DIBS."

"No, ME! I called dibs!"

"I called dibs on the YOUNG one. HE was SO CUTE."

"Did you see that IAN? I call dibs on HIM!"

"I'M going after that BARTENDER. The HANDSOME one from MO'S!"

Annie continued the poem in her head. *Beware the Jabberwock, my son! The jaws that bite, the claws that catch! Beware the Jubjub bird, and shun the frumious Bandersnatch!*

Henrie handed Annie a cup of coffee. She nodded her thanks and set it down on the small table on the far side of the room. She picked up a plate and perused Henrie's spread, settling on the sweet potato hash and chilaquiles. Every now and then, she turned to smile at the ever-talking women, nodding or shaking her head as seemed appropriate.

"WE have to go SET UP today. I'll bet we see LOTS of MEN at the PARK."

"I'll bet we'll hear GOSSIP, too! About the MURDER!"

Annie and Henrie looked at one another, both giving a small shake of their heads. The women were making it up as they went along. Annie turned back to the table to pick up a bagel. The poem continued in her head. *He took his vorpal sword in hand; long time the manxome foe he sought, so rested he by the Tumtum tree and stood awhile in thought.*

As she moved to the table at the end of the room, she felt a paw on her foot. She looked down. Tiger Lily's paw and face were her only visible parts. The rest of her was under the detective table. She looked up at Annie in what seemed to be sheer panic. She bent down to whisper, "It's okay, darlin' girl. When I finish breakfast, we'll leave."

Tiger Lily drew back into the detective agency, and Annie continued the poem in her head. *And, as in uffish thought he stood, the Jabberwock, with eyes of flame, came whiffling through the tulgey wood, and burbled as it came!*

Henrie, very unlike Henrie, brought a cup of coffee to Annie's small table and sat with her. Behind them, they heard the continuous stream.

"HANNAH, did you bring your PAINTS in? I'll HELP you take them OVER to the PARK."

"You can't help HANNAH! ALL of OUR stuff is in the TRUNK."

"We SHIPPED our BOOKS. They should BE THERE already."

Annie started the poem again. *One, two! One, two! And through and through the vorpal blade went snicker-snack! He left it dead, and with its head he went galumphing back.*

"Hurry UP, girls! We have to GO!"

"We're not FINISHED! This is a GREAT BREAKFAST!"

"I want some more of that FRENCH TOAST casserole."

"Get me a BAGEL, okay?"

Annie smiled at Henrie. She continued, in her mind, to recite, *And hast thou slain the Jabberwock? Come to my arms, my beamish boy! O frabjous day! Callooh! Callay!" He chortled in his joy.*

The women got up as one. "ANNIE, PROMISE to put in a GOOD WORD to that HANDSOME GUY. I want to PARTY with him before I GO!"

Annie smiled. They left. Annie turned to Henrie. Out loud, she said, *"'Twas brillig, and the slithy toves did gyre and gimble in the wabe. All mimsy were the borogoves, and the mome raths outgrabe."*

Henrie replied, *"I shall be telling this with a sigh somewhere ages and ages hence: two roads diverged in a wood, and I – I took the one less traveled by, and that has made all the difference."*

They smiled at one another, both realizing that they were very much alike, after all.

Tiger Lily poked her head out, wondering if the silence would be permanent. Annie looked at her and said, "Come on. Gather your siblings. Let's go to work."

At the Café, Annie listened with half an ear while patrons got the story of the night before half right and half wrong. WQVX had garbled the message, as usual, but the paper was close to the mark.

Chris came in for lunch with Ray. Chris carried a heavy box that he put on the floor behind the hostess stand. Jock settled in beside the box and looked up at Tiger Lily.

"What's in the box?" asked Annie. She had come from behind the coffee bar for a quick hug and kiss.

"Pumpkins. Pete and Janet's. I dropped yours and Henrie's at the Inn. I liked yours, by the way. Very nice."

"Were you surprised?"

"Frankly, yes…"

When she had time, she sat with them, taking a few bites of salad at a time. On her last visit to the table, she stood to go back to work but stopped. "By the way, Chris, I'm supposed to convince you to party with the women at the Inn."

"Do you really want me to?"

"What do you think?"

"Um…I'm thinkin' you would rather I either keep my distance or hang out on the third floor?"

"Good call, sailor."

Annie went to the server station and pushed the bussing cart to the dining room floor. She saw and overheard as Geraldine waved the paper at her table of friends. "They can't get anything right! Look at this. They claim that Laila and her kids are Hindu, not Muslim. Someone needs to set them straight!"

One friend said, "But what do they say about Mem and Frank? The news on TV said they were beaten half to death."

Another said, "They say it's the mob. I'll bet Frank launders money for them."

"I'll bet Mem does, too! She hangs out with all the wrong sort of people."

Annie approached the table. "Can I take some of these dirty dishes? Good morning, Geraldine. You look so pretty today. Is that a new dress?"

"Oh, stop it. I'm tired of how sweet you've become. What do you have to say about Mem and Frank?"

"Well, I happen to know that the paper got it right, mostly. The men were there because of Mem's ex-husband, and he seems to have disappeared."

"Ex-husband? Dennis?"

"You know him?"

"Of course. He and Mem were, well, they were not a good match. Dennis had ambition. He always had a great deal going on and she was always such a stick-in-the-mud. He made a lot of money, you know."

"I understand he lost a lot of money as well."

"Well, he was never a good manager. And Mem didn't support him like she should have."

"You mean financially?"

"No, I mean, well, you know what I mean. The way a woman should support her husband. She should never have divorced him. But she did, and he lost his way. I saw him the other evening. He hasn't disappeared. He's staying here in town somewhere."

"He was staying at the state park. His cabin is empty. The police are looking for him."

"Why?"

"They seem to think that the men who held Mem and Frank hostage were trying to get money from Dennis. Must have been another one of those, what did you call it? One of his 'great deals'?"

Geraldine huffed.

"Oh, I'm sure you'll be happy to hear that neither were injured badly. Diana's boyfriend interrupted them. They'll both be home from the hospital today."

Geraldine huffed again. "I'm sure we're all happy to hear that."

Annie moved on. She had done everything she meant to do. Said everything that needed to be said. Geraldine and her crowd would believe what they wanted, but at least the information had been given to them.

Pete and Cyril came in for lunch. Cyril ducked behind the hostess stand while Pete sat with Chris and Ray. Several people got up to walk over and ask Pete what was happening. Annie realized she could wait, even though she was bursting to know what Pete knew.

She looked behind the hostess stand. Cyril was certainly filling in Tiger Lily and Jock. If only they could speak human.

Billy and his crew met again in the safety of the stinking boat. Billy wanted to give his orders for the night.

Porter was the last to arrive. He put a large, dirty canvas bag on the floor.

"Ya got 'em?"

"Yeah. Had one of my boys at school go in. He got hold of four bats an' a hockey stick."

Billy stared at Porter. "And now someone else knows what we're gonna do."

Porter stared back at Billy, mouth agape. He swallowed hard. "No! Honest to gosh! I didn't tell 'im nothin'!"

"But when he hears about this, then he'll know."

"How was I supposed to get 'em?"

"You was supposed to go steal 'em from the box store."

"When? How? I ain't good at that stuff!" Porter pointed at the other three. "You coulda had one a them do it!"

Justin, Marc and Dallas looked at one another. Then they looked at the floor.

"Whatsa matter, boys? Gonna wimp out on me?"

The three looked at each other again before Justin finally spoke for the group. "We were talkin'..."

"Talkin'? You three? Without me?"

"Well, you know, we were walkin' over here, and we were talkin' on the way, and we were gonna talk to you."

Dallas and Marc nodded, both at Billy and at Justin for encouragement.

Justin continued. "We were thinkin' that there might be, you know, police there in the park. You know, since we were so good at the other jobs..."

Marc added, "And we didn't know nothin' about stealin' no bats and stuff..."

"And, well, we were thinkin' that maybe we've done enough. For now."

131

"Crisesake. We ain't done enough. We're gonna do this one last thing, then we can be done. For now."

Billy looked at Porter for encouragement. As always, when Billy argued with the other three, Porter sank into himself, looking from Billy to the group, Billy to the group. When Billy caught his eye, Porter nodded his head in a crazy, yeah boss, whatever you say boss, way.

Billy sighed. "Looka here. One more thing, then we're done. We're gonna go into the community building. There's a loose window in the back. Nobody's gonna see us."

Billy laid out the plan. Only Porter met his eyes, but Billy knew they would all be there. They didn't have anywhere else to be.

Justin ditched Marc and Dallas. He wanted to walk home by way of The Avenue. And then, maybe he'd go home, change clothes and look for a job. No, wait. Maybe he should change clothes first, then walk by the flower shop, then look for a job. Or change clothes, look for a job, then….

By the time he had it straight in his head what order he would follow, he had chickened out on everything.

14

Before Chris, Pete and Ray got up to leave, the Palindrome Gals came in for lunch. Annie caught Chris's eye. She gave him a wicked smile.

"OH! LOOK who's HERE!"

"HI, HANDSOME!"

"We REALLY wanted you to COME OVER last night!"

"WHY don't you INTRODUCE us to your FRIENDS?"

"We LOVE men in UNIFORMS!"

Pete and Ray had heard enough the night before. Both of them wiggled ring fingers in the air and got up to leave.

"Taken," said Pete. "My loss, I'm sure."

"I'm with him," added Ray. "My loss. Chris, see you later, buddy."

Annie stopped Pete at the door. "What's going on, Pete? I couldn't get to you for the crowd."

"Nothing, Annie. They're gone. Dennis is gone. No one knows anything, no one saw anything. We can't even find the park manager."

"The park manager is missing?"

"We don't know. His staff said he sometimes goes out into the park early in the morning to take a look around, and he sometimes forgets his radio. They say he lives in a state of – they called it 'perpetual confusion' – anyway, he is kind of a ditz."

"What about the cameras that Jolly put up behind the building?"

"They aren't as good as yours, so the men are just blurry images. Mem and Frank haven't talked to us yet, but Harrison gave us a broad description. It's a good thing he went to check on them."

"And you're sure they're coming home today?"

"Yep. They're coming to the station to give their statements in fifteen minutes or so. I'll tell them you asked about them. They'll call you if they need anything."

"Thanks, Pete."

Annie gave Cyril and Jock pets on the head as the boys left with their humans. Tiger Lily inched out from behind the hostess stand to rub against Annie's ankles. Annie looked down at her. "They're okay, darlin'. They're okay. We'll go over and see Mem later today. Just to make sure."

Tiger Lily followed Annie to the coffee bar and darted behind it. She curled into a ball out of the way of Trudie's feet and hid from the Palindrome Gals. Annie picked up their coffee orders and headed for their table. They had pulled extra chairs up to gather around Chris.

She could barely make herself heard, but she finally figured out who had which coffee, placed the cups on the table, and made sure the server was able to take their order.

Chris had finally said something that got through to them. When Annie returned to the coffee bar, she turned to see five women staring at her. The table was silent. For once. Hannah finally said, "ANNIE, YOU got yourself ONE HUNK of a GUY. YOU GO, girl!"

Chris looked embarrassed and relieved at the same time.

At the Inn, Henrie pulled out the rolling cart and took it to the porch just in time for Ramon and his friends – the band members of Bergamasco – to pull into the driveway.

Bergamasco had played in Chelsea the summer before, but they did not stay at the Inn. Ramon introduced his band mates and allowed Henrie to sort out the room situation.

Kali was in heaven. She loved men, and here were several. Both Kali and Ko were happy to see Fiamma, the large, flirty Bergamasco dog. Fiamma and Ramon resembled one another. He had dreadlocks that he pulled back from his face. She had dreadlocks and mats that covered everything, including her eyes. She had a fetching way of tossing them aside when large male dogs were present.

Henrie offered his signature tour as he turned names over in his head. He knew which rooms to assign, but apparently not everyone had arrived.

"Jules, you and Noelle will be on the second floor, in a room that faces the winery and the carriage house. Will she arrive today?"

"She's supposed to be here sometime tonight, Henrie. I appreciate that you were able to give us a room."

"I was happy to accommodate you, and very happy that you booked the rooms before the last set of guests. Had you booked later, the room would not have been available."

"We have Ramon to thank for that. He knew you would be full."

Henrie nodded and looked at the rest of the group. "Now let me see. I believe Manny and BeeBop will take the lower level of the carriage house, and I am to deliver your instruments and equipment to the top floor?"

Grip answered. "Yep. It was worth it to us to book the extra room."

Ramon said, "You don't need to worry about the equipment, Henrie. We'll take it. I almost didn't' get the extra room. Thought we would just let things stay at the winery. After seeing the building across the street, I'm glad we got it."

Henrie nodded. With the recent vandalism, he agreed. He left the group to deliver their luggage. BeeBop went with him, carrying a few cases that wouldn't fit on the luggage cart. On their way back, Henrie heard, "THIS place is FULL of HANDSOME MEN!"

BeeBop broke into a trot, while Henrie continued a sedate pace. He was in no rush to see this. Before he got to the porch, Ramon hurried out, gave a wave and said, "See ya later, Henrie!" He was followed quickly by Jules, "Want to see how the winery can be set up," and Manny, "I think I'll go to the Café and say hello to Trudie."

In the foyer, five Palindrome girls stared balefully at BeeBop, who tried his best to flirt with all of them at once. He was failing miserably.

James and Ginger were in the car again, headed home and feeling a definite lack of sleep. Ginger yawned. "Maybe we should sleep in our own beds tonight. And I really do need to study."

James responded to her yawn first, with one of his own. "But I know they're going to be out there. Certainly by tonight. They're going to start setting up for the OktoberFest today, at least some of the things."

"And they'll have security there. We can let it go for now. And Dad said there were mob guys hanging out at the state park. I don't think it will be safe."

James, peeved, turned his eyes to the road but continued to think about the night. He could go out on his own. The mob guys were after Mem's ex-husband. They wouldn't pay any attention to a teenager sleeping out.

Ginger was saying something.

"What?"

"Do you think you did well on your test?"

"I did okay. Could have done better. I can pull up the grade during the rest of the semester."

"That's going to be hard to do. It's settled. We'll stay home tonight, study, and get a good night's sleep."

"Yeah." James continued to think about getting out of the house after his mother went to bed.

"I'm sorry, man. I did everything I could, called in every favor. We just didn't ask in time. No one's available."

Ian hung up from his call, sighed, put the phone in his pocket and stretched his body, as much to relieve the tension in his mind as the tension in his muscles.

The security service would be unable to send officers tonight. Ian had moved budget items here and there until he found enough money to cover the extra night, but…no one was available.

Ian walked through the city park and went into the community building. The CanStruction projects were nearly complete. He strolled through, taking a look at the work.

Judges from the food pantry stood in the back of the room. They didn't want to start looking at the projects until the stated judging time arrived. Some groups were still putting on their finishing touches.

As Ian walked through the building, behind and to his left he heard a loud CRASH, then silence, then some very loud voices. He didn't turn around. He looked at his watch. They had twenty minutes to repair the damage, a little more if they weren't the first group to be judged.

When he reached the judges, he shook the hands of the volunteer staff – they were all volunteers, except for the director – then pulled the director aside.

"I tried to get some extra security in for tonight, you know, with all the vandalism going on."

"Oh, Ian, no one will bother us here. The doors will be locked when we leave; no one cares about this."

"I hope not. Just wanted to let you know we tried."

"Thanks, Ian. Hey, want to stick around for the judging?"

"No, thanks, I have to check in with some other folks."

Ian walked out the back door and moved to the area that housed three large vendor tents. Most of the vendors had begun to set up tables and chairs.

Vendors were set up outside the gated area of the festival and would open at eight o'clock in the morning. This was the first year the committee paid for vendor tents, and it seemed to be a good investment. The number of vendors booking space on the lakefront in October had almost doubled.

As Ian walked through, he stopped to tell the few vendors that were still there about the lack of security. Most people had the same kind of reply as Cici Dunlap, who worked with metal and had several pieces on sale.

"Ian, this is Chelsea. Nothing's going to happen. I never worried about leaving my stuff out, even in those years you didn't have tents."

The owners of the pony farm – they would have rides for children on Friday and Saturday – were finishing their fencing and putting out hay and water troughs.

"Hey, there, Ian. Good to see you."

"It's good to have you back again, Mr. Forester. How many ponies are you bringing this year?"

"We have ten of the nicest, gentlest Shetland ponies you ever did see."

"I broke my arm once, falling off a Shetland pony. He wasn't that gentle, as I recall."

Mr. Forester chuckled. "You told me that story last year. Don't know as I believe it this year neither."

Ian walked past the face painting display, and the jewelry display from that fair trade group, and the book sellers. They were set up, ready for business, but the women he met at the Winery were long gone.

Too bad. Attractive women. But loud. Really, really loud. Probably best he didn't hook up with any of them.

By the time Ian reached the end of the third tent, he was near the carnival area that took up part of the beach. Rides were in various stages of completion. Some were just pieces of metal on the ground, some were partially up, and one, the Tilt-A-Whirl, was completed. The games were up and ready to go, also, but the doors and windows were shuttered and locked.

Ian heard a group of voices…yes…the women were there. With a bunch of carnival people.

He walked around the basketball shoot game, and there they were. Several coolers had been pulled into a circle, and as Ian watched, a man got up, opened his cooler, and pulled out three bottles of beer.

The Palindrome Gals were having a great time sharing the largesse.

"IAN! Come on OVER here!"

"Have a BEER!"

"We've been LOOKING for you!"

Ian smiled, waved off the offer of a beer and continued past the group to a camper sitting in the back. He knocked on the door. It was opened by a woman in flamboyant dress – not very much on the top half. Ian always enjoyed the view.

"Long time no see, my handsome boy. Come on in here."

Ian went up the two steps and entered. Ms. Flamboyant enveloped him in a hug and kissed him on the neck, behind the ears and around his cheeks. She would have gone on forever, but they heard a man walk from the back of the trailer.

Ian extricated himself from the embrace and wiped lipstick off his neck. He was grateful to see the man.

"Have you heard about the vandalism we've been having around town, Mr. Flam...Gruber?"

"Yes. I saw evidence of it when we went to the Café for lunch. Too bad. Too bad. What's the world coming to?"

This from a man that Ian knew to bilk young children out of their hard-earned allowance at the Basketball Shoot and every other game on site.

"Well, as you and I both know, the world can sometimes be a hard place."

"That is so, my boy. That is so. But, you came to tell us this?"

"I came to tell you I tried to get some additional security, something to start tonight, but I didn't get it done. You might want to lock up extra tight tonight and have some of your people look around every now and then."

"Thank you, my boy. That, I will do. Now sit. Have some vodka."

Ian smiled. "Sorry, Mr. Gruber, Mrs. Gruber. I have other people to talk to this evening. See you tomorrow."

Ms. Flamboyant gave him a finger wave. "Come back when you can stay longer, handsome."

Ian had one last stop to make. He walked to Mo's Tap, gave a wave to George, Georgia and Candice, and found the person he was looking for.

He slipped into a booth at the back of the room and said, "Hilly, what's going on?"

15

Tiger Lily pushed a few paper butterflies out of the way and ducked under the tablecloth to enjoy a treat from Henrie. Mexican themed, of course. Taco meat topped with grated cheese. The cats finished and settled in to clean themselves up.

Tiger Lily looked around. *"Where are Mo and Mr. Bean?"*

Kali answered. *"They're hiding upstairs in the apartment."*

"What from?"

"It's who. They're hiding from those women. They can't keep their hands off them, and they're scared."

"Who ate their snacks?"

Ko turned her back on the group as she continued to clean up.

A little head poked its way into the agency.

"Um, I'm Daryll?"

Little Socks answered. *"Yeah. We know that."*

Tiger Lily bopped her on the nose. *"What's up, Daryll?"*

"Um, I can't find my human?"

Most of the cats stood up quickly, except for Ko, who struggled to get out of Kali's way. She was feeling a bit rotund.

Tiger Lily looked at Daryll closely. The little cat was filthy. *"When did you see him last?"*

"Um, early yesterday evening? I went out to, you know, take care of business? And when I got back, he was gone?"

"What happened?"

"*Um, I heard those men again? They were fighting with that guy named Dennis? And I think they beat him up? And while I was running back? I heard my human telling them to stop?*"

"*Then what?*"

"*They started running? All of them? Except that Dennis guy? I was scared? So I hid under a bush?*"

"*What did you find when you came out?*"

"*I think my human got away? I saw him at the cabin? But he just ran in, and then he ran out? He was carrying stuff? A bag with stuff?*"

"*And he just left you?*"

"*No? He called me? But I was scared? And I stayed where I was? He ran away?*"

"*That was last night?*"

"*Yeah?*"

"*Where have you been since then?*"

"*Um, I've been hiding?*"

"*You look like you've been on the run. You need a good cleaning.*"

Daryll looked at himself, then all at once he was even more embarrassed. A tear trickled down his face.

"*Don't cry,*" said Tiger Lily. "*Get busy, guys. Help Daryll clean up. I'll go see if Henrie has more snacks.*"

Sassy Pants took his head and ears; Ko worked on his back and sides; Kali performed a feat of acrobatics and worked on his stomach. Little Socks closed her eyes to take a nap.

Tiger Lily trotted into the kitchen where Henrie sat with a cup of coffee. He had the morning paper in his hands.

Tiger Lily stood and tapped Henrie's knee. Henrie looked down and she motioned to the dining room with her head. Apparently he didn't understand her, so she got down and started to walk that way, stopping to look back.

Henrie put the paper down and followed her into the dining room. Tiger Lily pulled the tablecloth aside.

Henrie leaned down. He saw the little cat from before, dirty, but getting a good cleaning up from several of the kids.

He looked at Tiger Lily. "She must be hungry."

Tiger Lily blinked once.

"I will get something that is not as rich as the snack you enjoyed. Some cat food, I think. Will that be appropriate?"

Tiger Lily blinked once again.

Henrie smiled down at her and went to the kitchen, returning very soon with a small dish of cat food and another filled with water.

He sat those within reach of the small cat and looked again at Tiger Lily. "I trust you will assure this food is still in the dish when the little one is ready to eat."

Tiger Lily positioned herself next to the dish and glared at Ko, who had made a step or two in that direction. Ko sat back down with a huff.

When Daryll was clean, Tiger Lily encouraged him to eat. *"You eat all of this, but take it slow. If you eat fast, you'll get sick. I'm going to try to read the paper, and I'll be right back."*

Tiger Lily found the paper where Henrie left it and jumped to the table to read. The front page story was about Mem and Frank. She read slowly, taking in all that she could understand. Some information was given about Dennis and the park manager. They didn't seem to think he was missing, though, only that he couldn't be reached for questioning.

By the time Tiger Lily returned, Daryll had finished and was cleaning up. *"The only thing the paper said about your human is that they're trying to find him for questioning, but he's missing. Cyril didn't know anything more than that."*

"So nobody knows anything?"

"Not yet. And they can't find Dennis, either. When did you see him last?"

"Well, um, it sounded like they beat him up? I stayed in the bushes for a long time after my human left? And those men? And then he came out? He was pretty beat up? And he limped real bad? But he drug a bag? And I heard a car start in the lot? And drive away?"

"So he really is gone, not laying out there in the woods somewhere."

"Um, I guess so?"

"Did those men come back?"

"Um, yes? They went into the cabin and said some really bad words? And then they left? I listened, but I didn't hear another car?"

The cats were silent. Then a very soft voice said, *"Um, Tiger Lily?"*

"*Yes, Daryll?*"

"*Um, do I have to go back to the park tonight?*"

The cats considered the implications of his question.

"*Can he stays wit us?*"

"*Yeah, Tiger Lily! Can he stay?*"

"*I think Mommy will probably let you stay here tonight. Well, until your human gets back, at least. She's done that before.*"

"*Really?*"

"*I think so. When we go upstairs, you just come with us. By the time she figures out there's one extra, she won't make you go.*"

"*Really?*"

Little Socks huffed, "*Really! Now go to sleep!*"

16

Annie called the cats upstairs for supper, poured cat food into several dishes, freshened up the water bowls and ran into her bedroom to change clothes. She was late to meet Laila, Felicity and Candice at Mo's.

She hurried out and glanced at the pile of cats sleeping in the dining room. "I'm late, kids. I'll see you later."

She turned to leave but turned back, wondering what she had seen. By the time she turned around, Tiger Lily had shifted in the pile, throwing an arm over, was that Sassy Pants? Oh, well, she thought.

She was out the door in a flash.

When Annie reached Mo's, the table was set. Three women sat in front of four tequila flights. Each flight contained six small glasses of tequila.

"I don't know about this," said Annie. "A margarita flight is one thing, but tequila? Shots? Someone is going to have to carry me home."

"These are only half shots," said Laila. "Look. Baby shot glasses."

Annie looked. They were baby glasses. "But altogether, they make up three shots."

"Yes. Three. You can handle three."

"I don't know…."

Laila said, "Come on, Annie. This is unusual for me to be out at night, and you promised me…"

"I did. I know. You can carry me home. Did you order food?"

In answer, a server set down four plates, forks and napkins and set a tray of appetizers in the middle of the table.

"What is this, Sarah?"

"Baby stuffed poblanos with walnut sauce, baby red chili enchiladas, and baby tacos."

"Everything baby."

"They're appetizers. Do you want a menu?"

"No. I think just this, but with all this tequila, how about another order of the same thing? In about fifteen minutes?"

"Sure thing. Here's the sheet that tells you about the tequila."

Annie looked at it and around the table at her friends. "Want me to read?"

"Let me," said Felicity. "You skip over the good parts."

Annie handed her the sheet. "Okay," Felicity read, "they have three types of flights to choose from. The vertical flight is three products from the same brand of tequila. The horizontal flight is three of the same type of tequila, but different brands. The Spirits of Mexico flight has six products of tequila and agave that are all made in Mexico, but they are different types."

"Which one did we get?"

"Guess. First of all, this is Mexican month. Second, did you count your glasses?"

"The Spirits of Mexico."

"Right!"

"Let me tell you first about tequila."

"Are you really going to read every word?"

"Most of them. Shut up and let me get started. 'Tequila is made from one species of agave, primarily in the arid lowlands and rainy highlands outside of Guadalajara, in the state of Jalisco. By law, it can also be produced in parts of four other Mexican states.'"

"There are laws?"

"There are laws. 'When the agaves reach maturity after several years, the sugar-rich hearts are cooked and crushed; the extracted juice is then fermented and, finally, distilled.'"

Felicity read on, silently. Out loud, she said, "I'm not going to read most of this. But this part is important. 'Never buy tequila that's not labeled one hundred percent agave.' I never look. I'm going to, now."

She read on. "'Blanco is the clear tequila as it comes off the still, though it can spend up to two months aging in oak barrels. Golden reposado is aged from two months to a year. Dark añejo sits from between one and three years, and the relatively recent extra-añejo is any tequila aged more than three years, which results in qualities similar to those of long-aged rums and brandies.'"

"Are we to the part yet that we can start to drink?"

"Yes. First glass on your left. Salud!"

"Salud!" The women reached for and tasted the first glass. Annie put the glass down after one taste.

Felicity took a taste, then said, "First, I'm going to tell you the cost. I'm not sure where they priced these, but anyway, this one sells for thirty-nine dollars. This is Herradura." She read from the sheet. "'Continuously

150

produced since 1870, it contains twenty-five million agaves, and the company uses agave propagated from the original plants.' Wow. From 1870. There is a lot more information here about making this tequila, but I'm going to pull an 'Annie' and not read it. We're drinking their silver, but they make others."

"Good, but expensive," said Laila.

"You ain't heard nothin' yet. Second glass, this one sells for fifty dollars. It's Siete Leguas. They use a process to crush the agave that they call 'donkey-pulled tahonas – stone-wheel mills.' I wonder if they still use donkeys? Anyway, this is 'a very complex process,' and they say we might taste spearmint, pine, earth and cinnamon."

Felicity stopped to taste the second one. Everyone else had already done so and pronounced it good. Annie, ever mindful that this was tequila, again drank only half of her half shot.

Annie looked around the room to clear her head. The bar was filling up; only a few chairs at the bar remained. As Annie looked, one of the chairs was taken by a woman that Annie didn't know. She was dressed in an overly elegant manner for Mo's.

Annie's attention was drawn back to her own table. Candice had taken the sheet and was saying, "The third one sells for fifty-three dollars. It's Casa Noble, and they call this 'a lowland tequila.' This particular one is called Jóven. It sits in 'an oak container for only six weeks, which makes it – technically – a blanco,' but it is different than their other blanco. You can taste something like dark chocolate."

Annie almost drank the entire shot, but remembered to stop – in time. She thought, I can go back to this one. If I'm feeling okay.

Candice looked at Laila. "The fourth one is more expensive. It sells for sixty dollars a bottle."

"I'll never drink anything that costs that much again, so let me at it."

"This is Fortaleza, now in its fifth generation of ownership. This is another lowlands tequila. The agave takes longer to ripen and is typically sweeter, like coconut.'"

Annie tasted it. She liked the chocolate one better, but this was good, too. She stopped at half of a half.

"Hang onto your hat, Laila. This next one is Patrón, the same brand we can find on local shelves, but this is their top shelf. It sells for two hundred ten dollars."

"No!"

"Yes. It's 'triple-distilled blanco. Smooth but with a spicy finish.'"

Even Annie drank the entire shot of this one. "Really? George put out shots of a two hundred dollar tequila? What did these flights cost?"

"Don't ask."

"This is just number five. How much does the last one cost?"

"Three hundred two dollars a bottle."

"No!"

Laila said, "Let me at it!"

Annie asked again, "How much did this flight cost?"

"Let it go, Annie. This is the only time you will ever do this."

"You're right. What kind is this? What makes it worth three hundred dollars?"

"This is good. You'll love it." Candice read from the sheet. "'Casa Dragones Tequila Jóven, made by Bertha González Nieves, the first woman given Maestra Tequilera status by the Mexican government.'" She looked at the group. "Clearly, both Mexico and Bertha broke with tradition." She read from the sheet again. "'This tequila goes through an elaborate modern multiple-distillation process. The process eliminates impurities and harsh flavors, then it adds some extra añejo.'"

Candice read silently, then said, "Bertha uses handblown bottles with hand-numbered, signed labels. 'This is the premium to end all premiums.'"

Once again, Annie drank the entire shot, thinking this is the shot to end all tequila shots for me tonight. I'm going to have to talk to George about this.

After six half shots of tequila, the women were loose enough to talk about all kinds of things.

Felicity wondered aloud, "I wonder if Trudie is going to get lucky tonight."

"Where is she?"

"She's at Clara's. They're having dinner with the band, and she got really dressed up."

"For Manny?"

"When will she ever learn?"

Annie said, "Look behind me. Is there still a pretty woman at the bar? Dressed really nice?"

Laila had a good view. "She's still there. I saw her come in. She keeps looking over here."

"Over here? Who is she?"

Candice said, "I've noticed her, too. She's not just looking at us; she's looking all over the room. But her eyes do seem to stop here more often than at other tables."

"Does anyone know her?"

Felicity turned around.

"Stop that!"

"I had to look, didn't I? And no, I don't know her. She must be one of the vendors or something at the OktoberFest."

"You're probably right."

Annie pointed to a corner table, where Geraldine sat with…him. "Have you seen this? Did you know?"

"It's been going on for a while, Annie."

"Yeah. You're just finding out?"

"Well, apparently, what happens at Mo's stays at Mo's, and no one told me. I need to come here more often."

"I hear Everett finally got wind of it. He asked Greg about moving into that apartment he uses whenever they're separated, but it's rented out to someone else."

"They can't afford to live together. How will they pay for two places?"

"Well, they might not. I heard him tell one of his friends that he's staying in the spare bedroom. Maybe they'll just live together. Separately."

"But why him? He's such a…such a…"

"Scag. Just say it, Annie. He's a scag."

Annie had history with this scag. This scag was Dan Tapper. Roving reporter extraordinaire. Idiot. News mugger. Fake news purveyor.

"I should go over and talk to them."

"No, you should not. And Laila, you stay away, too. The newspaper had a field day with his report about you, and they finally issued a retraction."

"They did? When?"

"On the noon news, at the end of the report, one time. I only know about it because it was on the paper's webfeed."

"Well, I should go over there and give him a piece of my mind." Laila put her purse on top of the table and started to get up. Annie on one side and Candice on the other stopped her.

"Give it up."

"Be the bigger person."

"Send him a box of dog poop."

"Wear gloves, and send it from somewhere far away from here. Not Marsh Haven. Maybe go to another state."

"Don't wear your dupatta. Put on jeans and a t-shirt."

"And get a wig."

"Wear glasses."

By now, they were laughing, and thoughts of getting back at Dan Tapper melted away.

Annie's back arched when she heard, "Let's have a PARTY TONIGHT!"

"I'm BEAT!"

"They have TEQUILA flights!"

"BRING us some of THOSE!"

155

Annie decided this was the perfect time to go. "I need to get home. Tomorrow will be a very long day." She and Laila left together.

Trudie finished setting the table while Clara put the finishing touches on her Cuban dinner. Noelle had finally arrived, and she laughed with the rest of the band as they told her about the Palindrome Gals.

BeeBop, who had a sense of humor about his lack of connection with the fairer sex, said, "You woulda thought, man, that I coulda gotten at least one of them interested in me. I mean, I'm not bad to look at, am I?"

"No, man."

"Do I smell? Have bad breath?"

"We've been over this a hundred times. You're cool. You just, you know, give off a vibe or something. It's like you need the women to like you, and they don't want to be needed like that."

"Don't try so hard."

"You've said that before. I don't think I'm trying…"

"Don't even say hello. Just, you know, hang back. Look at other things. Play hard to get."

"For how long?"

"As long as it takes."

Trudie listened closely, seeming to pay attention only to the table as she arranged Ropa Viejo and Picadillo, fresh fruit and Cuban-style rice and beans. That's what she needed to do. She needed to ignore Manny, for as long as it took. Even if it meant she didn't speak to him for the rest of the weekend.

And that's what she did. She laughed and talked with
Clara and Noelle, with Ramon and Jules, even with
BeeBop and Fiamma. With Manny, she glanced his way
only when he made comments to the full group. It wasn't a
full-on ignore. It was an I'm-not-as-interested-in-you-as-
you-think ignore.

She allowed Bee-Bop to walk her to the bottom of the
stairs of her apartment at the end of the evening.

When Annie got home, she realized that it might be a
long evening as well.

Henrie served coffee and tea to a group of people in the
foyer. Annie looked around, and after close to three shots
of tequila, she was still able to extend a polite hello to Ian,
Hilly, Boone, and a couple of town councilmen, both of
whom Annie knew by face and name, but not more than
that.

"What's up, guys?"

Ian smiled. It was a tired smile. It was an isn't-this-
festival-over-yet kind of a smile. The kind of smile she was
used to seeing when a festival had not yet started, but was
getting ready to tank.

Hilly stepped in. "Well, Annie, we needed to have a
little meeting of the committee because there is a…well,
there's a little…um…Boone?"

Boone leaned forward. "We have a problem with the
parade, Annie, and we kind of need your help."

"My help?"

Hilly tried again. "Yes, Annie. Your help. You see,
um…it appears that…well…Boone?"

"What Hilly's trying to say, Annie, is that the parade sponsor, the people that were going to pay all the extra expenses for the parade? You know, for the trophies, and the grandstand and sound system rental, and...well...they weren't too happy about what's been going on in town...and they backed out."

One of the councilmen leaned forward. "We thought, Ms. Mack, that you might be able to, as it were, fill in the gaps of our financial situation."

The other councilman leaned forward. "Of course, if you were to assist in this, um, endeavor, we would want you to be on the grandstand. Act as the grand marshal of the parade."

Annie turned back to the first man as he said, "Give out the prizes."

Then the second. "Sit right there beside Dan Tapper as he broadcasts the parade from the stage."

Annie looked over at Henrie, who had taken a seat with a cup of tea. His eyes went wide – briefly – and she could see the smile that threatened to erupt on his face. He was able to contain it, however.

The two councilmen continued their dog and pony show. "Kind of do a back and forth commentary with him. You know. Local color and all."

The two councilmen leaned back.

Annie's friends covered their mouths with their hands. Ian had a small cough. Hilly had a need to wipe her lips with a napkin. Boone tapped his fist against his mouth, as if fighting a huge tickle. Henrie sipped tea.

"And you're asking me because..."

The councilmen looked around at the group and realized it would be up to them. The first one leaned forward again. "Well, Ms. Mack, because of your position in the community, of course."

The second man rose to the occasion. "You are so highly thought of, and you are known to be a...a...a problem solver."

"Yes. A problem solver. That's exactly it."

Annie allowed the silence to linger for a few seconds before speaking. "And, besides the honor of working with Mr. Tapper, how much of a problem is it?"

"Excuse me?"

"The problem. How much are you asking me to, um, contribute?"

The councilmen again looked around at the group and realized it would be up to them. The second councilman gave Annie a figure.

Annie coughed, started to speak, coughed again, and took the glass of water from an ever-watchful Henrie.

She looked at the two councilmen. "Is that tax deductible, gentlemen?"

They smiled, sat back and nodded, all at the same time. They were very coordinated.

James went to the same clump of small trees that he had used before. On the lake side of the community building, they hid a small, flat space large enough for one small adult to lie down or for two small adults to sit. The trees offered privacy from people who might approach from any direction, but James could position himself to see the community building or any other part of the park.

James had napped in his bedroom, setting his alarm for midnight. When the alarm went off, he checked to make sure his mother was home. She was. And safely in bed.

He walked out the back, where a sleeping bag, an extra blanket, gloves, a hat and a flashlight were hidden. Now safely in the trees, he put himself into a comfortable sitting position and kept an eye out for trouble.

He heard what sounded like a herd of elephants around two o'clock. He looked out, and sure enough, it was the bully boys. In the dark, he could distinguish five shapes. He thought they would go for the easy damage, maybe the vendor tents, or the pony ride, set up but empty of ponies for the time being. Or even the carnival area. They could break out some lights over there.

The boys didn't go to those places. They circled the community building, coming very close to James in the process. He shrank back, staying low and putting a tree in between him and the boys. They were looking for something. He heard a person he thought to be Billy say, "Here. This is it. Just pop it out. The wood is loose."

James heard some grunts and a crack, then what sounded like glass breaking. He heard the boys scramble into the building, then he saw the lights of the building come on.

The sounds were awful, and they went on forever. James knew what was inside. The can projects. He had touched almost every single one of those cans, and they were supposed to go to the food pantry.

He felt sick, but he scrambled as far away from the community building as he could, moving further into the trees as he brought out his phone.

Moving backward quickly, he started to dial nine-one-one, but he tripped over something. He fell backward, hitting his head against a rock on the ground.

James didn't know how long he had been unconscious. He could still hear the bully boys in the community building, but it sounded like they were almost finished. There were more silences than there were cracks of what could be ball bats against cans. He reached around himself on the ground for his phone.

Before finishing his nine-one-one call, James used the flashlight app to see what he had tripped over. When he saw it, he dropped the phone and started to scream. He screamed and screamed.

17

Pete looked at the display on his cellphone. It was almost time for the alarm to go off, but he still had a few good minutes of sleep left. This had better be good. "Yeah."

"Chief, we need you at the park. Some festival people found a couple of bodies by the community building."

Pete was wide awake now. "What? Bodies?"

"Well, one body and someone headed to the hospital. He's in pretty bad shape."

"On my way."

At the park, Pete looked at the photograph of the young man headed to the hospital. He picked up his phone and dialed. When Janet answered, he said, "Don't ask, just go. Check Ginger's room. Make sure she's there."

When Janet came back on the line to assure him Ginger was there, he heaved a sigh of relief. "That's good. James was in the park. He's on the way to the hospital. I have to tell Laila. Do you think you can go over and stay with her other kids?"

Arrangements made, Pete then walked to the body, still face down on the ground. An officer showed Pete the driver license pulled from his back pocket. "Looks like it's Mr. Stimson, Pete. He works at the state park. He's the manager."

Pete watched as one of his officers "bagged and tagged" a baseball bat. He then stuck his head into the community building, but he didn't enter. The dozen or so CanStruction displays were a mass of spilled food items among dented and broken cans. Thousands of dollars of canned goods destined for the food pantry had been destroyed.

Before leaving to talk to Laila, Pete called his dispatcher. He was done waiting for evidence to pick up the bully boys. He ordered part-time and reserve officers to every location the boys could possibly be found: their homes, their hang-outs, the few places that a parent or two went to work.

Those boys were going to be charged with murder.

Kali and Ko were the first to arrive downstairs. They saw Pete in the kitchen, in front of the monitor. While he watched the video feed, he told Henrie and Mommy about an incident in the park.

While Ko stayed behind with Cyril to listen, Kali ran upstairs to tell Tiger Lily. And Daryll.

Daryll stood in shock. Tiger Lily moved directly in front of him. *"Daryll! Daryll! Look at me!"*

Slowly, Daryll pulled Tiger Lily into focus.

"My human? My human is dead?"

"Let's go downstairs and see what we can find out. You're here with us, Daryll. You're safe. This is bad news, but we'll help you get through it."

The cats went downstairs halfway in between their normal fast and a sedate slow. Mo and Mr. Bean hung back, looking around for the women. They wanted to get underneath the detective table and into a back corner without being seen.

Annie barely registered the cats' entrance into the dining room, and she didn't notice the extra one that stuck close to Tiger Lily.

"I've got to go to the hospital, kids. James was hurt."

The cats heard, "WHAT were all the SIRENS, Henrie?" and dove for cover.

Back at the town park, Pete tried to contain his anger while he conferred with his officers and the Sheriff, who had come in with a coroner.

"I saw the boys head down The Avenue toward the park. I was able to follow them almost all the way to the park entrance. The time seems right, early in the morning, and I was able to identify the five I know. They carried bats, and one had a hockey stick. I wonder if that was what got Mr. Stimson. He wasn't beaten with a bat."

The Sheriff said, "No, it wasn't a hockey stick. He'd been beaten, but the coroner said it was probably with fists. When we rolled him over, we saw a gunshot wound. That's probably what killed him."

"Those boys are carrying guns now? That's not good."

"Pete, don't jump to conclusions. These are two different types of things. It looks like they beat the boy after they destroyed those cans. There's evidence of food embedded in his injuries. They probably saw him and beat him up a bit, not enough to kill him, just break a few bones, and they knocked him out. But this man, now he was killed deliberately."

"It coulda been my daughter."

"You're still pretty worked up, Pete. You ought to let us take lead on this."

"It's my case."

The Sheriff stared at Pete. They had worked together for several years and there was mutual respect. The Sheriff finally said, "Okay. It's your case, Pete. But if I tell you to back off, you'd better do it, and do it fast."

Pete looked him in the eyes. "I'll do it."

Off to the side, far enough to be out of the crime scene but close enough to catch Pete and the others with the camera, Dan Tapper gave an on-site report.

Henrie and the women watched on television. Henrie had a small television in the dining room for days such as this, when the guests would have an interest in local news. For once, the dining room was silent with the exception of the news report. Henrie moved around the table, filling coffee cups or juice glasses, taking a used plate or utensil.

Dan Tapper was, well, Dan Tapper.

"Once again, we are first on the scene of a brutal incident in Chelsea. Charles, I have to say that it's becoming more and more typical of this town to have brutal, agonizing crimes. Earlier this week, a terrorist attack was made on a Muslim woman just up the street."

Charles, shown on half the screen, broke in. "You're right, Dan. There have been several incidents. I understand that woman is of the Hindu…"

"Muslim, Hindu, one and the same, Charles. This town is under siege. Today, I'm at the town park. Behind me and to my left, you can see the community building. Inside this building there were – let me check my notes – it looks like thirteen CanStruction projects. You can call them CanDestruction projects today. They were sculptures put together by community volunteers, Charles. Volunteers! These were statues made out of cans of food. Thousands of dollars of food, Charles, ruined. These canned goods were destined for the food pantry. Instead, it's a massive mess. Unfortunately, we don't have footage of that. It's a crime scene. We can't get in.

"You can see, behind me and to my right," Dan turned, to make sure Pete and the others were still there. They had moved out of camera range. "I'm sorry, Charles, they're no longer there. Town and county police officers and the county coroner are investigating a brutal murder, possibly two."

"Two murders, Dan? We understand a victim was transported to the hospital…"

"Yes, Charles. One of the two victims. I understand the victim that was transported was a Muslim."

"WAS a Muslim, Dan?"

"We have no idea if this person is still living."

"But you have the identity of the victim?"

"We do not, Charles, but we understand the victim is a relative of the Muslim woman involved in the terrorist attack…"

The screen cut to Charles Veritone. "It appears our live feed was lost. That was Dan Tapper, our on-site reporter. Let me repeat what he had to say. One victim, as yet unidentified, has been transported to the hospital. His condition is unknown at this time."

Henrie walked back to the kitchen. He heard, "TWO people KILLED." "A TERRORIST attack?" "On MUSLIMS?" "We HAVE to go LOOK at our SET-UP." "Do you want to LEAVE?" "We HAVE to STAY. I NEED the MONEY." "TWO people were KILLED!" "TERRORISTS!"

He was too tired to correct their impressions.

He felt some energy return, however, as the band members filed in. They filled plates and accepted coffee or juice from Henrie while Noelle introduced herself. She was obviously used to meeting women who loved to meet band members. Henrie stifled a smile when he heard, "I understand you've met my husband, Jules." She placed an emphasis on the word 'husband.' "I'm Noelle. So pleased to meet you."

Five sets of batting eyelashes redirected toward Manny. BeeBop tried manfully to gain attention but was summarily rebuffed.

Annie pulled out of the driveway in a car owned by the Inn. As anxious as she was to get to Laila, she first parked at the corner and walked back to the yoga studio.

Diana sat at the counter, eyes red, face puffy. Harrison Jones sat behind her. Over Diana's head, he nodded at Annie.

Annie walked over quietly. "Diana, I just wanted to make sure you were okay."

"Oh, Annie," Diana sniffled. "I'm okay. It wasn't Dad, anyway. But that poor man. Surely he was one of Dad's victims, just like Mom and Frank."

"Certainly your dad didn't do it…"

"No, but he's running from the men that probably did. I hope he didn't have anything to do with hurting James."

"Do you want to call someone else in today? Close up?"

"No, I'm fine. Really. I'll finish my cry and my cup of tea, and I'll be okay. But if I need to, thanks for the permission."

"Alright. I'm going across the street for a minute, then to the hospital. If you need me, just call."

Annie walked across to CyberHealth. Mem was stoic behind the counter. Her left eye was a purplish yellow color, and a bandage covered part of her forehead on the right side. Her left arm was in a sling.

Even with her injuries from the night before last, the only sign of distress that Annie could see was the slight wobble of the hand holding a cup of tea.

Annie went behind the counter, and as Mem set her tea on the counter, Annie wrapped her carefully in a hug. They stood that way for a long time.

Mem broke the hug. "Go. Tell Laila I'm thinking of her."

Annie nodded and left.

18

Ian was in fairly good humor for a man whose festival got started with the loss of a sponsor, vandalism and a murder. Pete released the park to the OktoberFest committee by noon. By then, Ian had dozens of volunteers ready to go to work.

Ian and George talked as they set up the beer tent – which was supposed to have been a beer area inside the community building – next to cordoned-off CanStruction projects.

George had only one complaint. "You know those keg toss people aren't going to be at all happy that we had to cancel their event."

"What would you rather do with the space? Have a two-hour keg toss or a two-day beer tent?"

George, struggling with cases of beer that needed to be iced, said, "You know the answer to that. Say, how bad is it in there?"

"It's awful. And it's beginning to stink. Tuna, salmon, corn, tomatoes, every kind of bean known to man...I'm glad to be helping you instead of cleaning up in there."

"It's too bad about the food pantry..."

"The festival insurance should cover that loss. It'll end up being a blessing for Laila. She'll purchase the same amount of canned goods for a second time. And be paid the second time. She can probably use the financial help. This is the second time James has been beat up in just a few months. That kid isn't living right."

"And I always thought he was so quiet. He just ends up in the wrong place at the wrong time. Hey, did you see the sculptures?"

"Yeah. The judging was done yesterday. They took pictures of all of them, and I think they're going to put up a display board somewhere. The pictures will be posted with the name of the groups that made them, and the winners."

"Who won?"

"I don't remember the group, but it was the Angry Birds display. They had a tipsy-looking thing with five pigs of different sizes, and three of the birds. One was set up in a slingshot – The Blues – and they had the end result getting ready to blast into the thing. You know, the three smaller blues. And Red and Chuck were standing ready."

"Which one is Chuck?"

"The yellow one shaped like a triangle."

"Tetrahedron."

"Yeah. That. Do you play?"

"Only when I'm waiting for Candice to buy shoes. So when I play, it can be for hours. How did they make those little blues?"

"They used tuna cans with blue labels suspended by coat hangers. I think they used those sticky picture hangers somehow."

"I wanted to get in to see them. Candice's alumni group did one. They made the snowman from *Frozen*."

"Olaf. That was a good one. They had a snow fort, some snowballs, and the foot of the snow monster coming in from the side."

"It took them a night to cover all their cans in white paper."

By this time, they were ready to set up the keg for the opening ceremony. Even though it was Mexican month on The Avenue, the beer for the Fest was German.

"Which one of these do you want to open with?"

"The Bitburger."

Ian looked through the kegs to find the right one. He took a stab at pronouncing the others. "Er-dinger, Francis-caner..."

"Fron-shis-conner."

"Whatever. Paul-aner."

"Close enough."

Ian answered his cellphone. It was Felicity. She asked, "When are you going to open the festival?"

"It's not two yet. What's the rush?"

"The public lot is full, people are wandering up and down The Avenue, they're taking up table space and buying nothing. Paying customers are walking away!"

"Okay. We're close enough. They can come in, we just won't tap the keg until two. Make the announcement up there; we'll do it down here, too."

Ian's security guards – unfortunately unavailable until today – opened up the barriers behind the vendor tents, and the crowd surged into the park and onto the beach.

The beer tent filled up, and so did the carnival area. German music piped through the loudspeakers and a festival atmosphere blossomed.

From tragedy to joviality. Just like that.

Ian stood inside the tent opening as beer drinkers entered in a steady stream. When a break in the crowd appeared, he stuck his head outside the tent to see what the crowd looked like. He moved back out of the way as a teenager entered the tent, tuba straddling his shoulders.

"Hey, man, where are we supposed to set up? Behind the bar?"

"You wish, my teenaged friend. You wish." Ian pointed him over to a corner and watched as the high school pep band set up. The students – mostly the boys – looked with longing at the kegs of beer behind the bar, while the band director, principal and two volunteer chaperones fussed about. They tuned up, and the director looked at his watch. It was two o'clock.

Ian pointed to George, who had already put on the official medallion, a huge thing that covered his entire chest. In a loud voice, and with a very bad German accent, George said, "Welcome, one and all to the Chelsea OktoberFest! I am your Burgermeister!"

The crowd, now filling the tent to standing room only, applauded and made catcalls.

George continued. "A Burgermeister is supposed to be the mayor of the town, but here in Chelsea, we have no mayor. I am the next best thing. A bartender!"

He bowed to applause and more catcalls.

George introduced Ian as OktoberFest coordinator, then turned the microphone over to the band director.

"Good afternoon! We're happy to be here this afternoon, and I assure you, we will be outside the tent before this keg is tapped."

A few boos could be heard from the band.

"We will perform the national anthem and then a medley – a short medley, I know you didn't come for the music – of German drinking songs and polkas."

The crowd listened in reverence, most with hands over their hearts, as the national anthem was played. They waved their arms and tapped their feet to the German medley. Ian realized that most of the people in the tent had been drinking already. Probably since sometime this morning.

The band finished to much applause – as much as coming closer to the opening of the keg and free beer for all as for the music – and the Burgermeister once again took the microphone.

George waited until the kids left the tent, surrounded by anxious adults, then turned to the crowd. "Many Burgermeisters choose to quote Martin Luther, the leader of the Protestant Reformation, who had a great quote about beer drinkers entering straight into heaven. I, however, choose to quote Plato, the classical Greek philosopher, who said, simply, 'He was a wise man who invented beer.' I hereby tap this here keg!"

Cheers and shouts of "Let the drinking begin!" could be heard at Tiger Lily's Café.

Henrie walked out to the porch. A rocking chair looked particularly comfortable, so he sat. And rocked. Kali napped on a chair near the railing while Ko curled up on the table at his right hand.

He looked toward the park and the beach. Cars continued to pull into the municipal lot, and people continued to enter the festival.

The beer tent had been his responsibility. As soon as George became aware of the vandalism in the community building, his first call was to Henrie.

"Need your help, Henrie! I've got to get this beer together, but we need a tent. And a bar. And I don't know what else."

Henrie had called upon his extensive knowledge of community resources...and called Harry.

Harry, one of the drivers for a rental company in Marsh Haven, was particularly fond of Chelsea. He found a tent, a bar, folding tables, chairs, keg coolers and a couple of German-looking six-foot-tall beer steins.

His loaded truck arrived at noon, to the relief of George, Ian and beer lovers everywhere, and the OktoberFest was saved. At least the beer part.

Henrie didn't break a sweat, but he planned to take George up on his offer of dinner for two at any restaurant, anywhere in the state, sometime in the next six months, please, but not around Christmas. And please keep your drinks to a minimum.

German music wafted on the breeze, getting tangled up with the ongoing music of the carnival. Henrie liked to hear a good German band, and he liked carnival music, but not necessarily at the same time.

Annie had called to tell him that James was in an induced coma. His condition was critical but stable. There was nothing to be done but stand by in the event Laila needed assistance.

Ginger was with the other children. That, too, had been arranged by Henrie. A quick call to Janet, and Ginger suddenly had something to occupy her mind rather than to worry about James continually. And Laila's younger children looked forward to the carnival rides Ginger had promised.

Henrie lapsed into thought. He smiled when he thought about Annie's predicament, being asked to pay an outrageous sum for the privilege of spending a few hours with Dan Tapper. Of all people.

Then his eyes moved across The Avenue, to the still visible destruction from earlier in the week. He hoped the insurance company would come through quickly. Fat chance, he thought.

Well, the day was moving on, and he had responsibilities. Henrie rose, two cats half rose and stretched, and eventually, they went inside.

Henrie sat down at the computer in the kitchen, opened the cupboard door, and leaned back in his chair while he fiddled with the remote control.

All he really wanted to do was assure himself that he could operate the system, and that he could tell one camera feed from the other. His training had consisted of watching Pete operate the monitor early this morning.

He pushed something, and the video scrolled backward at a high rate of speed for quite a while before he figured it out.

There. He got it.

Henrie looked up. The time and date stamps told him that these images were captured last night. He figured out "play," and watched for a while, amused. He saw the Palindrome Gals enter Mo's Tap. He watched Ian and the others walk toward the Inn, wanting nothing more than to get money from Annie. He watched them enter.

He saw Annie and Laila leave Mo's Tap. They gave one another a friendly hug, and Laila walked across The Avenue. Annie worked hard at walking a straight line toward the Inn.

Henrie chuckled. Then he sat up straight.

A woman followed Annie out of the bar. She was tall and slender. She wore a pencil thin dress and a cardigan with a hood. Very chic. She stood on the sidewalk and watched Annie walk toward the Inn. Using each camera feed, Henrie could tell that she watched until Annie was inside. Then she went back into the Tap.

Henrie fast forwarded, slowly. After a time, she left the Tap and walked to the Winery. She left the Winery as it closed, chatting amiably with other patrons as she walked to her car.

Henrie watched until her car, driving toward the town circle, was gone from view.

He sat back.

What was she doing here, and why had she not let him know she was in town?

19

Pete's officers found the five boys. While George tapped the keg in the park, the bully boys sat in a holding cell. Billy had just been returned to the cell following questioning.

Dallas, Justin and Marc sat on the bunk that took up much of one wall. Billy shoved Porter out of the way and sprawled on the opposite bunk, taking up all of the available space. Porter moved to the front of the cell. He sat on the floor and leaned against the bars.

"I didn't tell 'em nothin'. Keep yer mouths shut when they take ya."

Porter asked, "Ya mean nothin' nothin', or lie?"

"Nothin'. You tell 'em you want an attorney. An' if they say you ain't bein' charged with anythin' yet, so you don't get a free attorney, then you tell 'em you still ain't sayin' nothin'."

Marc whispered, "What about that guy? Did they say anything about that guy?"

"Shut up about that!" hissed Billy. "They got cameras and shit in here!"

"What if they have, you know, fingerprints?" asked Justin, keeping his voice low.

"I ain't even talkin' to you. What'd ya do that for?"

Justin looked at the floor. Marc and Dallas looked at one another, then at the floor.

"I said, what'd ya do that for?"

"So now you're talkin' to me?"

"Fer crisesake. Stay outa my face."

Billy had one more thing to say. "One of you dunderbutts left a bat. I hope whoever it was wore gloves." Billy didn't add that he thought the bat might be his. It was probably the bat Justin had knocked out of his hands after he hit that nerd a few times.

Billy laid back and closed his eyes. He could hear the three idiots whispering, but he couldn't make out what they were saying. They were wimping out on him, and Justin was leading the way.

They had fun when all they were doing was dumping trash and smashing crap. They had begun to whimper when Billy brought out the spray paint for the building on The Avenue. He'd had to force them to go to the park last night. He was the only one with the guts to beat up that little crappy kid, and then Justin had to knock the bat out of his hands! Fer crisesake!

Billy rubbed his arm. Justin's bat didn't break his arm, but he sure had a bruise. What nerve. He was in charge, not Justin. He called the shots, not Justin.

And then, they saw the body. Fer crisesake! A body! Right there. And no one had seen it. Not until he'd hit the kid a few times and Justin knocked the bat out of his hands. Then Porter shined his flashlight around to see what had made the kid scream.

A body. What rotten luck.

Billy made a fist and pounded the brick wall. Ouch! He tried to rub his hand without letting the crew know he had hurt himself.

The police had asked him about the body. They asked him about the bat. They asked him about the crappy kid, and the cans, and the food, and all of the other crap they'd been doing. But they had nothing on him. Nothing. So what some camera caught him walking to the park. That's not a crime. They had nothing. Unless his prints were on that bat. If they were, he was in deep crap.

His old man had better get down here and bail him out. Except the cop told him he was being held for questioning. No bail. Not yet. Not until he was charged. The cop said it like he was definitely going to be charged. With something.

No more juvie. The world considered him to be an adult now. What rotten luck.

Justin took his turn in the interview room. He wasn't surprised to see his questioner would be the Chief of Police himself. After listening to his rights – again – Justin declined the offer of an attorney.

"Son, you want to tell me what happened out there?"

"I'll tell you, sir."

"Go ahead. I'll stop you if I have questions."

Justin told him everything. He started with Billy's release from the juvenile facility when he turned eighteen and ended with the night before, when he took his own bat to Billy to stop the assault."

"You hit Billy?"

"Take a look at his right arm. It has to be bruised. Upper arm."

Justin watched as the Chief took out his phone and sent a text message to someone.

"So why do you hang out with him? With them?"

"I haven't got a clue. I want out. I wanted out in high school. I wanted out when…well…when…I'm real sorry what I tried to do to your daughter and all."

"Save it. Are you willing to testify at whatever trials come up because of this?"

"Yes, sir."

"Are you willing to plead guilty to any charges that come your way?"

"Yes, sir."

"There could be jail time involved."

"Yes, sir."

Justin sat, looking at the table, waiting for the Chief to tell him how long it would be before he set foot in the world again. Waiting for the Chief to tell him just how low he had sunk. Waiting to see just how bad a person he had become in his eighteen short years of life.

His head shot up when he heard Pete's cellphone ring. He listened to the Chief's half of the conversation. "…induced coma … the other guy? … gunshot? … so it wasn't the kids … estimate on cans? … that much? … bad bruise? … get him to the hospital for ex-ray … okay, thanks."

Justin watched as the Chief stood. He couldn't help it. When the Chief said his next words, Justin broke down in tears.

Ian walked through the OktoberFest. For the next two hours, he stopped to talk to someone at each demonstration booth. Over fifty groups and individuals signed up to provide food, soft drinks, ice cream, baked goods, Tupperware, make-up, jewelry, clothing, household items, wooden furniture, posters, and wall hangings. In some booths, artists showed their work and created pieces on site.

He watched toddlers, teens and adults line up to get their faces painted and watched characters walk away. The Wolverine, Elsa, Wonder Woman, Mulan, Batman. Others walked away with butterflies, flowers or dramatic lines on their faces, or masks of indeterminate vintage.

He was intrigued with the work. Hannah mistook his interest as intrigue for her. She fluttered her eyelids and her hands in his direction in between faces.

Ian noticed, but he waved and moved on.

At Anna and Eve's jewelry booth, he picked up a bracelet made of multi-colored glass beads. As he held it in his hand, holding it up to the sunlight to watch the light shimmer through, Anna approached.

"Isn't it pretty?" she asked. "Do you have someone in mind?"

Ian noticed that her voice was much more modulated when she was in sales mode than when she was in the group he met earlier in the week. Having noticed that, he turned slightly to look at Eve. She was talking to a customer and she, too, had a much softer voice.

He looked at Anna again. "No, I just thought it was pretty. What is it?"

"This is called Millefiori, or 'a thousand flowers.'"

"So, this is a fair trade company?"

Kathleen Thompson

"Yes. The proceeds support poor families in Nepal. Families that would otherwise be pressured to sell their children into brothels or other forms of child labor."

"That is really interesting." Ian stood there for a while, considering Anna. "Why don't we get together later? You can tell me more about it."

After making a date, Ian walked away. He stopped at several other booths and soon found himself in front of a bookstore. Nan and Emme greeted him warmly.

In the back of his mind, Ian noted softer, friendlier voices. He wished he had met these women, the intelligent-sounding ones, before meeting the high-octane, fun-loving ones.

There was still some high-octane. Nan said, "So, you're seeing Anna later, huh? Got any friends for me?"

Ian laughed. "No, sorry. So which one of you writes romances?"

Emme raised her hand. "Guilty. I write for Harlequin. Here's my latest."

Emme handed over a book with the picture of a buxom redhead in some kind of an embrace with the neck of a horse. It was very sexy. He decided he needed to move on to safer territory.

"So you, Nan, must write the mystery novels."

"I do. No romance there. Well, there's romance, but it doesn't get bogged down in those heated embraces."

"Do people die?"

"At least one per novel. But you don't feel the gore or the pain of it. You don't know until after the person is dead. Found. Or missing, presumed dead. Or…well, you know what I mean."

"I think so." A group of women stopped by and gave Ian the excuse he needed to nod and walk away. He heard the sound of a rock band and realized it was three o'clock. This band would play until six, then Bergamasco would start. They, however, would be behind the Winery, and activity at the park would start to wind down for the evening.

He realized it was time to check with his security detail and make sure they were prepared for the overnight shift. He continued his tour of the booths, stopping at each one, as he made his way toward the information and security tent.

Ian ducked into the tent and almost ran into Pete, who was ducking out. "Whoa!"

"Sorry, Ian. Just checking on the arrangements for the night."

Ian got on his knees in front of Cyril to offer a two-handed strokefest of head, around the ears, neck, back and chest. Cyril stood still for the love and wagged his appreciation as Ian finished.

"What have you found out, Pete? Did those boys kill the park manager? Is James going to be okay?"

"First, I don't think the boys did it, but I'm not telling them that. I'm letting them worry that they might be charged with murder. We're pretty sure that body just happened to be there. Maybe they pushed James back into the trees and he accidently ended up there, or, I don't know. It's a coincidence, and we don't like coincidences."

"What about James?"

"Last I heard, he's in critical but stable condition and in an induced coma. Upper right leg and lower left leg broken, one arm, a couple of ribs, and the doctor said he had two blows to the head, only one with what could have been a bat. So there's a concussion. I don't know how much other damage was done. They won't know until he wakes up."

Pete looked down at his feet and shuffled them.

"Is it possible that he won't wake up?"

"I don't know, Ian. I just don't know."

20

Annie heaved a sigh of relief. She had on short pants and sandals, allowing her feet to breathe in the night air, a sleeveless tank, a short sleeved flowing top, and a three-quarter sleeved floppy cardigan. Layers against the cool breeze, but not too much to make her hot.

She had left the house to the wailing of cats that sounded as if they were being cooked in hot oil. They knew she was going to meet Cyril and Jock, and they weren't invited.

And, darn them, they had adopted another cat!

Earlier this evening, as she got ready to leave, she looked in at the sleeping pile in the dining room. She saw a hind end that looked kind-of-but-not-quite like Sassy Pants. When she looked closer, Tiger Lily moved to sleep on top of the cat. But just then, she caught sight of Sassy Pants herself from the corner of her eye. She turned her head quickly, and yes! Sassy Pants was on the left side of the sleeping bundle of joys.

Annie had leaned in, moved Tiger Lily to one side, and picked up a small grown cat. He was pretty, and he looked scared. A little spot on his lower lip endeared him to her in a second.

"Who are you?" she had asked. "Do you have a name? Are you lost?"

Of course, the cat could not answer. At least, not in human words. He did manage a squeak.

She held the cat close, so he would know he need not be afraid, and she looked around at her seven. They were sitting up now. They looked her straight in the eye, as if to say, "He's ours now. You can't take him away."

"It's too late tonight, kids. You can keep him for now. Apparently, we've been feeding him for at least a day. I thought I saw an extra tail last night."

Annie returned the cat to the pile. "I'm going on a cruise with Cyril and Jock tonight. I'll tell them you said hello." She closed the door to the howls and gnashing of teeth that accompanied a mommy's-doing-a-mean-thing moment.

Now she sat on a comfortable chair, feet up, on the deck of The Escape. Chris was beside her, and on a table in between them was a chilling bottle of Pinot Gris, two glasses, and a small plate of cheese, crackers and nuts.

Pete and Janet sat in a similar setting a few feet to her left; Ray and Cheryl a few feet to Chris's right. Cyril and Jock sat at the railing, looking back toward the shore and the lights and activity at the city park and on the beach.

The motor was off; the lake was placid; the boat rocked lightly as the water moved peacefully beneath them. The air was rich with the scent of autumn on the lake.

They were far enough from shore to have lost some of the ambient lighting. A thousand stars shimmered in the sky. They would soon be lost, however, to the rising moon, almost full.

The group maintained a companionable silence. As they ate dinner in the galley earlier that evening, a subject would come up, but it wasn't pleasant. Then another. Same thing. And another.

Chris asked, "Have the boys been talking, Pete?"

In answer, he received a glare.

Ray asked, "Chris, are those women still after you?"

He received glares from both Chris and Annie.

Cheryl ventured, "It's good that Mem and Frank are home. Have you found the men who did it?"

Janet glared this time.

Pete asked if anyone was going to watch the parade. The sound of silence was deafening.

Annie did manage to make a point, that none of her guests were involved in this particular round of criminal activity.

Finally, Pete called a break. "We don't need to talk about a thing. Let's go look at the stars."

And they did.

Cyril and Jock sat at the railing, looking back toward the shore and the lights and activity at the city park and on the beach. They sighed. Often. Cyril finally said, *"Do you think they even realize Fiamma is in town?"*

"No. They don't care. They don't think about us when they make plans."

"It would be nice to see her."

"I think we're going to the Winery tomorrow to hear the band."

Cyril huffed. He hadn't heard any such thing from his human. It was possible they would be there. It was also possible Jock would have the lovely Fiamma all to himself.

Ian had been invited to join Anna for dinner at Bon Vivant. She insisted on paying. Normally, this invitation would have been a no-brainer for him, but tonight, he didn't feel so festive.

Ian's phone rang. When he answered, it was Anna.

"Hey, I know it's been a hard day for you. I heard you know that boy, and probably the man that was killed. I'm real sorry."

"Thanks, Anna. About tonight…"

"Oh, I know tonight might be tough for you, but, hey, you have to eat, don't you? And I'm paying. Just you and me. I'm going to ditch my friends for the night. Whadaya say?"

Ian thought about the now-soft-voiced Anna and the excellent meal he could expect at Bon Vivant. "Sure," he said. "What time?"

"Henrie suggested reservations, so I made one for seven o'clock. Will that work for you?"

"Sure. Want me to meet you there? Or I could meet you at the Inn and walk you up the street."

"Meet me there. Less of a possibility the others will tag along."

"Good point. I'll be there at seven."

Ian was about five minutes late. He found Anna at a table in the middle of the room. As he sat down, he said, "This is a great place during the day, and it's a different kind of great on the weekends. Have you seen the menu?"

"Yes. There are lots of Mexican options, keeping with the theme. I've actually picked out what I want already."

"Great. Take my card and order for me. It will be an adventure."

Anna turned their cards over to the server, who looked at them quickly. She said, "I'll be right back with those aperitifs."

And she was. On her tray were four small glasses. "For each of you, a shot of Herradura tequila, and to sip with it, Sangrita. This is a traditional Mexican blend of tomato, orange and lime juice, onions, salt and hot chili peppers. Believe it or not, the Sangrita is supposed to quench the fire of the tequila."

Ian laughed. "I wanted an adventure. Looks like I've got it!"

Anna laughed as well. "I made a rational decision on the wine this evening. It's a Casa Madero Shiraz."

"Excellent."

Ian and Anna talked and laughed through the appetizer, avocado stuffed with shrimp, and the soup, albondigas, Mexican meatball and vegetable soup.

Anna finished her soup. "I really don't need to eat this bread. I've done nothing but eat and drink all week."

"So you might need to soak up some of that leftover alcohol. This will be good for you."

Ian handed her the basket filled with green chili cheese beer bread… "I wonder if they used Mexican or German beer…" and Mexican monkey bread, made with cheddar cheese, peppers and parsley.

When the vegetable and starch dishes arrived, they were served a mixture of zucchini, onion, poblano peppers and corn, and a dish that looked like Mexican rice but tasted like rice cooked with pumpkin pie spices.

"Do you know the cook?"

"Sure," said Ian. "He's always willing to try something new, and there are a couple of women that cook with him, one in particular, that can outdo him. If she wants to."

"We haven't even gotten the entrée yet. I don't know if I'll be able to make it through."

"He cuts down the portion size of the entrée. Well, even though you've had all of these dishes, each one has been smaller than you'd expect."

"I almost said something with the salad, but then I remembered how many things I checked on the menu card."

"They allow plenty of time. They won't chase us away if we chew slowly."

And that's when the entrée arrived. Chicken with pumpkin seed-tomatillo sauce.

"The card said this version was somewhat Americanized. The chicken breast is grilled instead of boiled, but the sauce, it said, is the real deal."

"Do you remember what's in it?"

"Not everything, but pumpkin and sesame seeds, tomatillos, cilantro, onions, I think serrano chilies. And this is coriander on top."

Ian asked Anna how she got involved in the fair trade business. Anna asked Ian why he seemed to be so popular around town. Ian asked about the Palindrome Gals. Anna asked about Henrie. They were interrupted by the arrival of dessert.

Before Ian dipped his first mini pumpkin churro into the chocolate-coffee dipping sauce, he asked, "Why do you ask about Henrie?"

"Oh, he seems like such a nice guy. You know. Very formal. Seems to know what you want before you even want it. Slips in and out of rooms and you barely register his movements. Very handsome. And let me say that again. Very handsome. Is he single?"

Ian put his fork on his plate and looked at Anna. "We're pretty informal here in Chelsea, to the extent that we know a lot about everyone, we expect that everyone knows everything about us. We expect to have no secrets, if you know what I mean."

"Yes, I know what you mean. You seem so serious."

"When it comes to Henrie, we don't talk."

Anna looked at Ian with puzzled eyes. "You don't talk? About Henrie? Why not?"

"Henrie is different. He takes care of all of us at one time or another, in one way or another. He's a private man. We respect that."

Ian picked his fork up and took another bite.

Anna continued. "You know, there was a woman at Mo's last night, and she walked all over that bar asking questions about Henrie. I guess, more than anything else, that's why I asked."

"Who was the woman, and what kind of questions?"

Coffee appeared at the table.

"Um, I don't know who she was. Her skin was about the color of Henrie's, I'd say coffee-colored. Tall, slender, and she wore expensive clothes and shoes. Very tasteful jewelry."

"Did she seem to know people that were there?"

"I don't think so. She approached us just like she approached all the other tables."

"What did she say?"

"Let me think. We'd had quite a bit of beer earlier, and we were having tequila flights...she asked if we knew the man that worked at the Inn, and one of us said, 'Henrie?' and she said yes and asked us what we could tell her about him. And you know us, we just spouted off. You know, what a good cook he is, and a good host, and the Inn is so pretty, clean and well-run."

"Is that what she was looking for? That kind of information?"

"I think, maybe, but you know how loud we get when we're all together. She kind of wanted to move away from us."

Ian laughed. "I can't imagine why."

Ian thought about Mo's. He had been at Mo's earlier the night before, but he hadn't seen a woman of that description. He was troubled by news of this woman, but he didn't know why. Perhaps he should say something to Henrie.

Anna was talking to him. "...I can see you're tired. Walk me home. Then go home yourself. Get some rest."

As they walked down The Avenue, they could hear Bergamasco playing in the outside garden between Mo's and Sassy P's.

Anna said, "Sounds like a good band."

"They are good. They've played here before. The sax player actually lives here in town."

"Do you feel up to a song or two?"

"Sure. One or two. Then I'm going home."

Ian finally rolled into his own bed a few hours before dawn.

21

Henrie was up early Saturday. He was the only one.

The Palindrome Gals should have been up, had breakfast, and been ready to go to their booths by eight o'clock.

Eight o'clock came and went. So did eight thirty.

At nine, Hannah drug herself down the hallway and into the dining room.

"Good morning, Hannah. Did you sleep well?"

"Did you know that if you do lots of wine one night, and beer, then a tequila flight the next, that you had better stay away from alcohol the third night?"

"I had not given that particular idea much thought, but it does sound sensible. Will you allow me to make a plate for you?"

Hannah's voice was strained. "Please. I'll just sit here, hold my head in my hands, and, say, do you have a straw? I think the coffee will go down better with a straw."

"Certainly."

Henrie supplied the straw and dishes with small amounts of bland foods: oatmeal with cranberries and walnuts, topped with brown sugar, an English muffin with a side of honey, a slice of ham and cubed cantaloupe. He added a glass of chilled cranberry juice to her place setting.

"Thank you, Henrie."

"You are quite welcome."

Henrie returned to the kitchen to allow Hannah to eat – or not – in private. Soon, he heard the other women as they made their way into the dining room.

Walking back, he realized most were as full of remorse as Hannah. Anna, however, seemed calm. Quiet, but calm. She moved over to Henrie and whispered, "I'm the only one that didn't get snockered last night. Ian kept me sensible."

Henrie smiled. He provided straws for Emme, Eve and Nan without being asked, and placed filled plates and juice in front of them.

Eve groaned, "Henrie, what time does that parade start?"

"I believe it starts shortly, at ten o'clock."

"Oh, good golly, we've got to get going, girls."

"Okay. Are we ready?"

"I need more coffee."

Henrie retired to the kitchen. He reappeared at the door with a tray of thermal mugs. "Coffee is poured. Please add cream and sugar if you need it."

"Henrie, you're a peach."

Henrie smiled to himself as they trudged out the door. He had already arranged with the band members that they would have breakfast, billed to the Inn, at the Confectionary, because they would not be up until ten thirty or eleven.

All he had to do was clean up, and the rest of the day was his. What to do? What to do? Perhaps he should watch the parade, find a place somewhere close to the viewing stand. Make faces at Annie to add to her angst.

No. He would commiserate with her later. No need to put himself through the torture.

He decided to go to the private beach and read a book. And think. He had a lot of thinking to do.

Annie dressed to be seen on television. Which meant that she put on the same clothes she would have worn on any given Saturday.

She got to the parade review stand before Dan Tapper and his crew, so she decided to take the best seat. The one that would be in the warm sun for most of the parade. She carried a thermal container of water – one of those new-fangled ones made of aluminum that was supposed to keep cold things cold for twenty-four hours and hot things hot for twelve hours. Since Annie usually had room-temperature water, she assumed it wouldn't heat up in the sun for as long as she was there.

Ian jumped onto the review stand and sat beside her. "Is Henrie going to be here this morning?"

"I don't think so. He had a book in his hand and waved to me as he headed down the hall to the back porch. If I were a bettin' woman, which I'm not, but I'd win, I'd bet he's on the private beach with a comfortable beach chair, a chilled bottle of wine and a good book."

"But you ain't a bettin' woman."

"Nope. Not me. Did you need him for something? Can I help?"

"Well, I doubt it. You know how private he is?"

"Tell me about it. I live in the same house with him, and I don't even know what country he's from."

"Yeah. That's what I mean. I had dinner with Anna last night – you know, she sells jewelry?"

"Yes. How'd that go?"

"Very well, actually. She used her inside voice." Annie laughed. Ian continued. "She was at Mo's the night we all came to see you."

"Yes. I remember. They came in a little bit before I left."

"I was there a little earlier, but I left because, as you know, we had to have an emergency meeting. Anna told me about a woman who was asking everyone about Henrie."

"What?"

"Yeah. She described her, and I don't remember seeing her."

"What did she look like?"

"Tall, slender, attractive, expensive clothes, skin the color of Henrie's."

"I saw her. She came in somewhere in the middle of my tequila flight."

"Was she walking around, asking questions about Henrie?"

"No. She was sitting at the bar, looking around the room. We thought she looked at our table a little more than she looked at others."

"Maybe she knew who you were."

"But she was asking about Henrie. If she knew who I was, wouldn't I be the logical person to ask?"

"You're right. That doesn't make sense."

"Maybe I'll talk to Henrie later." Annie's thoughts went to the monitor. Maybe she could back up the video and show Henrie the woman that asked about him. She should be able to come close to the time the woman entered Mo's.

Tiger Lily and the kids were on the front porch. They had prime seats, either on the railing or on tables, putting them up high enough to see most of the parade.

"Why duzn't peoples watch from here?" asked Sassy Pants. *"We has da best seats in da town."*

"They can't see as well as we can. Believe it or not, from here to there, it's all blurry to them."

"There's Mommy!"

"She's the grand marshal."

"Wot's dat?"

"I think they just wanted to make her feel good about paying a lot of money for the parade. She gets to tell people about the floats and stuff."

"I heard she has to sit with that news guy."

"Yeah. Dan Tapper. Mommy thinks he's an idiot."

"So does everybody else we know. Do you think Mommy will break his nose again?"

"I think she'll be polite today. She's not the news, the parade is."

"Dis is gonna be fun!"

They moved over to make room for Fat Cat, Scaredy Cat and Tillie. Tillie, shocked to see a new face, said, *"Who are you?"*

Mr. Bean was embarrassed. *"I forgot to tell you we got a new kitty."*

"Really? Hello. I'm Tillie."

"Um, I'm Daryll?"

Fat Cat explained. *"Daryll lived at the state park, but he had some trouble, and now his human is dead."*

"That's the dead guy? Your human?"

"Um, yes?"

"I'm so sorry to hear that. You found a good home, that's for sure."

"Um, I don't know if I can stay?"

"Well, don't worry. She won't put you out. I was left here by some awful people, and Annie found me a home."

"Yeah," said Scaredy Cat. *"She found a home for us, too, and she let us stay here until our fur-evers were ready to say yes."*

"Fur-evers?"

"Yes. Annie found us a fur-ever home, a home where we can live fur-ever and ever."

"Me, too, and she still feeds us and stuff when we come over to visit. Well, mostly Henrie feeds us, but Annie has to agree, I think."

Daryll looked down at the floor. A tear rolled down his cheek. *"I used to have a fur-ever home."*

Tiger Lily moved close. *"And then, some bad people took that away from you. Mommy won't let that happen again."*

Tiger Lily looked around at the group. *"Speaking of that, we've been falling down on the job. James was hurt, Daryll's human was killed, all of this stuff has been happening on The*

Avenue and at the town park, and we haven't given a single clue to Pete. We need to get busy."

Little Socks said, *"Later. The parade is starting!"*

Tiger Lily thought to herself, it seems as if we only find clues if we have bad people at the Inn. We're going to have to get better, that's all.

Dan Tapper talked in a loud voice and waved his arms around, giving what seemed to be unnecessary instructions to his camera crew. Finally, he climbed the steps to the review stand.

"Well, I didn't expect to see you here."

"I'm sure you didn't. There was a last minute change."

"Oh. So, you're standing in for Mr. Jones from First Federal Bank?"

"Mr. Jones and First Federal Bank are no longer affiliated with this parade."

"Oh. I see. Well, let's talk about how we're going to do this."

"We're going to take turns reading and providing commentary."

"Well, Annie, that's not how…"

"That's how we're going to do it. Equal air time, Mr. Tapper. And you can refer to me as Ms. Mack."

"I've always…"

"Remember, Mr. Jones and First Federal are no longer affiliated with this parade. I am."

Dan coughed, turned around, and possibly made a face toward his camera crew, because he got a few laughs.

"Mr. Tapper, I will behave like an adult, a respectable, professional adult, and I expect the same in return."

"Oh, yes, right. Um, I need to check in with the station."

Dan motioned to his crew and placed an omnidirectional microphone on the table. To the side, his crew turned on a monitor, allowing Dan and Annie to see what the camera saw. After several seconds, the anchor, Charles Veritone, could be seen on the screen.

"Dan, are you ready to go? Is that…aren't you Annie Mack?"

"Yes, Mr. Veritone. You may refer to me as Ms. Mack during the broadcast."

"Certainly. I, uh, I'm just surprised. I thought we'd be seeing Chuck Jones."

Dan said, in a level tone, "Mr. Jones and First Federal Bank are no longer affiliated with the parade."

"I see. Well, have you had the talk, Dan? About who is doing what?"

"We have had the talk. Ms. Mack and I will share equally in the reading and commentary."

"You're…"

"Sharing equally in the reading and the commentary."

"I see. Well, let's do a microphone check."

22

Annie and Dan were keeping it as civil as they could, on air and on point.

Midway through the parade, Dan reminded the audiences – at the parade and at home via television – that a panel of judges had already chosen the winners.

"And here is the winner of Best Use Of Theme, the Alpha Chi Omega Sorority. It's all about the beer, folks! And the beauties! This Bavarian beer garden comes complete with patio tables and chairs. Beer drinkers raise their steins, and several sexy waitresses are on hand to service them. Great job, girls."

Annie said nothing about Dan's sexist remarks, thinking it would do no good, especially on air. She was supposed to be on her best behavior.

Annie was on the microphone when the next winner stopped at the review stand. "Give a round of applause to the winner of the Most Humorous award, the High School Cheerleaders. These young men and women are dressed as a cleaning crew on the morning after. Not only do they have to pick up overturned tables and chairs, but you'll notice several people in various stages of morning-after recovery. These teenagers are set to tackle everything, armed only with brooms, mops and dustpans."

Dan announced the next one. "This year, the football team received the Judges' Choice Award. These young men are charging to the goal posts with beer steins instead of footballs. They're making touchdowns. They're completing passes. They're getting three-point conversions. And their secret? They use only the best steins from Hamburg, Germany, courtesy of the football coach, who brought them home last summer." Dan turned to Annie. "Ms. Mack, do you think he emptied every one himself?"

Annie smiled and thought better of commenting on the drinking habits of the high school football coach. She moved on to the next entrant.

Eventually, not nearly soon enough for Annie, the last entrant passed the review stand. Dan looked into the camera and said, "And there you have it. The Chelsea OktoberFest Parade has chalked up another..."

"Just a minute, Mr. Tapper. We have one more award to give out."

Dan took a panicked look at his notes. "I don't, um..."

"The Grand Marshal's Award. This year, that award will go to the Chelsea Rotary Club. As you recall, their float featured several short Minions attempting to serve large steins of beer to people sitting at tables. Tables, Mr. Tapper, that were taller than the Minions. We saw some acrobatic jumps and falls being taken, and some of those Minions got pretty wet. Congratulations, Rotarians."

Annie smiled her most angelic smile into the camera, then turned to look at Dan. "Mr. Tapper, it's been a pleasure."

Dan's response was cut off as the station cut to Charles Veritone. "Thank you. That was Dan Tapper and Ms. Annie Mack at the Chelsea OktoberFest Parade. And now, let's take a look at the weather."

Dan's face got redder by the second. He sputtered more than he talked. "You...you...you did that on purpose!"

"What's that, Dan?"

"You added that award to steal screen time."

"Dan, I paid for this parade. If I wanted to add ten awards, I could have done it, and I don't care if we were on-screen or not. Suck it up."

As Annie prepared to leave the review stand, Ian climbed up. He brought out his cell phone. "Annie, Dan, I'd like to take a picture of the two of you."

Dan continued to sputter. "You...I'll...you..."

Annie's smile was beatific. "Yes, Dan?"

Dan's red face turned purple. Ian tried to capture the two together and set the camera phone to take pictures in bursts. They just wouldn't stand still.

Annie reached down to pick up her container of water, and as she came up, Dan's fist, apparently aiming for her nose, connected with the side of her head.

Annie acted on autopilot. Her right hand shot straight out, and the aluminum container connected with the front of Dan's nose. The crunch was more satisfying than the one she heard – and felt – a few months before.

Ian stared at his phone. He had captured it. Every second. Separate, high quality images, date and time stamped. This. Was. Wicked.

Harrison walked from the apartment to the yoga studio. Diana had just finished with a class.

"Diana, your mom's shop isn't open."

"What? Sure it is."

Diana looked across the street. One of Mem's regular customers had just tried the door, and she tried it again. She gazed into the window, using a hand to shield her eyes from the sun, shrugged her shoulders and walked away.

"Maybe she had to go upstairs for something."

"I was in the apartment all morning. She wasn't there. I went down the back way, didn't see her. I was all through the store. Came out the front door and let it lock behind me."

Diana turned to look at her students. "Jim, do you have time to stay here for a few minutes, while I go check on something?"

"Sure. Take your time. I'll even teach the next class if you don't get back."

Diana and Harrison crossed the street. Diana did what the customer had done. She tried the handle and looked through the window. Then she got out a key, opened the door and went in.

The shop hadn't been opened at all.

Frightened now, she grabbed her cell phone and tried Mem. No answer. She tried Frank. He answered on the first ring.

"Hello, Diana. What's up?"

"Frank, have you talked to Mom this morning?"

"Not since she left around seven or so. Is something wrong?"

"I don't know. The store's not open."

"Maybe she went upstairs."

"Harrison said no, but he just went back up to check again. It looks like she didn't even open up today."

Harrison came down, shaking his head.

"She's not in the apartment."

"You tried to call?"

"Sure I did, that's why I'm calling you."

"Stay there. I'll call Pete, and I'll be right over."

23

The parade was nearly over. Watching it from the porch – using cat and dog eyes – had been fun. Now, Sassy Pants jumped up and said, *"Brown Mousie! Wot you duz here?"*

Brown Mousie scurried up to the porch and onto a chair. He looked around, a bit frightened to be out in the open. He saw an unfamiliar face. That face looked at him with hunger.

"Who's that?" Brown Mousie pointed to Daryll.

"Dat's Daryll. Daryll, dis is Brown Mousie. We duzn't eat him. He's a friend."

Sassy Pants met Brown Mousie at the winery a couple of months before. For a while, the little mouse just chittered, allowing Sassy Pants to read his mind and translate to the group. As he grew more comfortable around the cats and dogs, he showed his skill of speaking real words.

Brown Mousie kept a wary eye on Daryll, but he said to the group, *"I thought Sassy Pants might come over today, even though it's Saturday, but…anyway, I heard something you might want to know."*

Tiger Lily came close. *"What did you hear?"*

"There was a man, he came in last night before the band got there, and he was talking on the telephone to some guy. He said he was going to get her today, and he'd hold onto her until her friends paid."

"Did you hear any names?"

"*Yeah. One time he said 'Mem.' I like Mem. She smells good. And one time he called the guy on the phone by name. He said Cooper.*"

"*Did anyone speak to the man? Call him by name?*"

"*Yeah. Some guy came over and said, 'Hey, Dennis, I heard you were in town.' And he left real quick after that.*"

Their attention turned to the street as Pete's police car blazed up The Avenue from the park, sirens on. It stopped across the street from Mem's place; Pete and Cyril jumped out.

Tiger Lily said, "*Little Socks, keep Cyril there as long as you can. I have to go downstairs and try to write these names.*"

Tiger Lily had managed a breakthrough in communicating with humans. While watching Annie's nieces and nephews play Candyland, she learned the letters and the sounds they made. Kind of. Annie and Henrie, in an effort to encourage her, left paper and edible paints in the basement, and three walls were covered with letters, pictures, words and sounds.

As Tiger Lily ran downstairs, she prayed that Ko hadn't eaten all the paint. She hadn't. There was still some red in the pot.

Tiger Lily grabbed the top sheet of paper, put it on the floor, and looked around for clues of how to spell "Dennis." She remembered reading his name in the newspaper, but she couldn't recall exactly how to spell it.

A small copy of a picture taken at the last block party was on the wall. It included Annie, Tiger Lily and all her siblings, Chris and Henrie. Underneath the picture, Annie had written, in plain block letters, "all of us." Annie had read it to Tiger Lily several times, pointing her fingers at each syllable.

Tiger Lily knew how to do the last of the name.

She slowed down her racing mind and concentrated, one picture at a time. Nothing led her to the first part of the name.

Well, she thought to herself, I'm going to have to figure it out myself.

Mr. Bean and Sassy Pants ran to the basement to join her.

"Duz you got it yet?"

"Can you spell it?"

"I'm going to have to make it up."

Tiger Lily focused on the letters. She settled on a "D," and after putting the tip of her paw in the paint pot, she made a long stick and a half circle meeting it on both ends.

She looked at the letters again, and settled on an "I." With her paw, she made a long stick. She then made an "N" with two straight sticks and an angled stick to connect them.

One more time, she looked at the photograph. She upended a "C" to make a "U," then she started the "S." *"This is one of the hardest ones to make."* She had to stop in the middle of the curves, dip her paw again, and finish it.

She sat back to look. It was an understandable "D-I-N-U-S."

"That will have to do."

Then she looked at the wall while thinking of the name Cooper. The first letter was easy. On a second sheet of paper, she made one straight and two angled lines. K.

She looked at the younger cats. *"I'm not sure how to spell the 'oo' sound."*

"Duzn't any of da letters makes dat sound?"

"Maybe that U one does. Mommy said sometimes letters make different sounds. She said English is hard."

Tiger Lily formed another U, thought about it, added a P, and sat back, befuddled. *"There has to be a way to spell 'er'!"*

"Dat's da last sound of part of your name."

"You're right! Thanks!" Tiger Lily finished the second sheet of paper. It now said "K-U-P-E-R."

Mr. Bean took one page in his teeth and struggled up the stairs with it, tearing one of the corners off in the process. Sassy Pants did the same with the second, but the tear in that page was a bit bigger. The page threatened to come apart.

Behind them, Tiger Lily called, *"Can you make it across the street?"*

The strong little kitten and the cat with ADHD nodded. Gamely, they ran with them to the foyer, out the door, and across the street.

By the time they got there, all of the cats and Tillie behind them, the papers were a bedraggled mess, with dirt marks, torn parts, several tooth marks and a few paw prints.

Not caring that people stared, they marched into CyberHealth, Tiger Lily and the rest on their heels, and sat down next to Little Socks and Cyril.

Pete heard some shuffling and turned to see all of the neighborhood cats surrounding Cyril. He noticed a new one. Mr. Bean and Sassy Pants had something torn and dirty in their mouths.

Pete, at first, turned back to the humans. Then he turned to look again. Tiger Lily was cleaning her front paw of something that looked like blood. He looked at the younger cats again. Those dirty pieces of paper had red paint on them.

Pete knew not to dismiss anything the cats and dogs might have to add to an investigation. He nodded to them to signal that he would be with them directly.

While the cats waited, Kali leaned over to whisper to Tiger Lily. *"Brown Mousie said there was a woman there this week asking questions about Henrie."*

Tiger Lily looked at her sharply. *"What?"*

"She went around to all the tables and asked about him, well, mostly him, and some about Mommy."

"What did she want to know?"

"If he and Mommy were dating, what kind of a man he was, that kind of thing."

"What did people say?"

"Brown Mousie said mostly nobody said much of anything, except maybe that if she needed to know something, maybe she should ask him."

Pete approached the group. He walked to Mr. Bean and Sassy Pants and got down on his knees. This was as much to shield what he was doing from the people in the room as to get down to their level.

Softly, he said, "What do you have here, Mr. Bean?"

Mr. Bean let go of the paper as soon as Pete touched it. Pete studied it, mulled it over in his head, then put the paper on the floor. He turned to Sassy Pants. "Will you let me look at this?"

Sassy Pants dropped the sheet to the floor. Pete studied and put it on the floor next to the first sheet.

He put his hands out and looked at Cyril. "Did Tiger Lily write this?"

Right paw to right hand, meaning "yes."

"Does this one say 'Dennis'?" "Yes."

"And this one says 'Cooper'?" "Yes."

"Do you know anything else?"

Cyril looked around at the cats, then put his right paw to left hand. "No."

Pete looked at Tiger Lily and gave her a solemn nod. He folded the papers and put them in his chest pocket before standing up to face the confused humans.

"Sorry about that. I wanted to make sure they understood this was a crime scene. You know. I told them not to move or touch anything." He looked at Diana. "Has your father contacted you, Diana?"

"No. I haven't heard from him since before, well, the incident. Mom surely would have said something if he got in touch with her."

"Do you know where he might be? Who his friends are?"

"If I knew, I'd tell you, but I don't know anything about him. When I was a kid, I didn't know who his friends were, much less, now."

"Does the name Cooper mean anything to you?"

"No. Nothing…."

Pete turned back to the cats and dogs. He wished they could tell him more, but from the looks on their faces, they knew no more than he. "Go on home, now. Except for you, Cyril. We've got work to do."

Pete thought about that name. Cooper. There was Angela Cooper, a school teacher. And Terry Cooper, who worked at the bank. At his office, he pulled out a telephone directory and found all the listings for Cooper. Only three in town, and the third one was a son – he thought it was a son – of the Cooper that worked at the bank. Unfortunately, cell phones didn't turn up in the directory, making searches in this day and age a little tough.

Marco passed the office doorway. "Hey, Marco, do you know anyone named Cooper?"

"No…well, yeah. There's a teacher and a guy at the bank."

"No one else comes to mind?"

"Well…." Marco squinted his eyes and looked up and to the left. He was thinking. "There was a guy…but I think he went to prison when I was in high school. You were in the Marines then. He lived out somewhere near, maybe even on the property of that marina that caters to the rougher element. You know the one. His family owned it before he went to prison. Maybe he still does. I didn't hear that he was released, but if he screwed up in prison and had to do all his time, he wouldn't have had a parole officer."

"So, no parole, no reason for us to know about it. That's always a comfort. Would you know him if you saw him?"

"Maybe. Why do you want to know?"

Pete realized he couldn't tell Marco why he was interested in someone named Cooper. The more he communicated with his animal friends about clues, the harder it was to communicate with humans.

"No reason. The name just came to me, is all."

Marco rolled his eyes and continued his walk down the hallway.

Pete looked at Cyril. "Come on. Let's take a ride."

Pete parked on a road just past the marina, and they walked in, keeping to the sides of dilapidated boats, trailers, trucks and cars. One area held several old trailers which could possibly still be used as homes. Hovels, more like it. It seemed strange to Pete that he had not been called here for one reason or another over the years.

Pete was frustrated. He couldn't knock on the door without reason, and there was no way to tell if Mem was in there. He finally looked down at Cyril, who had been prancing and whining for nearly a minute.

Against his better judgment, he said, "Go on. See if you can smell her."

Cyril got low on his legs, walked swiftly to the door of the first trailer and smelled long and hard. He went to the second, then then third. There, he stopped. He looked back at Pete and returned as quickly as he could, still staying low.

Pete put out his hands. "Is she in there?"

Tap to the right paw. "Yes."

Spirits were high in the beer tent. Ian arrived and showed the photos to George and the rest of the volunteers.

George pulled Ian behind the bar. "I have my laptop here. You know, point of sale stuff. Let's download those pictures just in case someone confiscates your phone."

While Ian took care of that, George got the crowd's attention. "I have something to celebrate! The next round's on me!"

After the round was out, George calculated what he owed the till. "Next time I'm gonna be a little more, what word would I use?"

Ian suggested, "Circumspect?"

"Yeah. That. Oh, well. This is one for the record books. You were in the right place at the right time, that's for sure. I'll bet the station comes after her this time."

"They probably will. Hey, look at these guys."

George looked. A group of well-muscled guys – George thought of steroids – came in. They wore khaki shorts and sleeveless muscle shirts – in October – and looked unhappy.

They came to the bar and approached George.

"You in charge?"

"Yeah. Can I help you?"

"We're here for the keg toss."

"Oh, sorry, man. That was cancelled, you see…"

"I paid the fee."

"Give me your name. I'll return…"

"My girl's here. She expects to see me win."

"Can't help you there, but if you…"

"You say you're gonna do somethin', you gotta do it."

"Are you going to let me talk?"

Out of the corner of his eye, George saw Ian move back and pull out his phone. He hoped Ian would call security, but he believed the phone was in camera mode.

"Okay. Talk. Tell me what I want to hear."

"I don't know what you want to hear, but we had a murder."

"A what?"

"A murder. And some serious vandalism, and this," George indicated the beer tent with his arms, "was supposed to be in another place. In the building that was hit by vandals. So the police told us we couldn't be there, and the only place we could be was where the keg toss was scheduled. Here."

"So you shoulda canceled the beer."

George looked around the tent. The beer drinkers were getting quiet, listening to the conversation.

"You think we should have cancelled the beer. For two days and two nights. Because of a two-hour keg toss."

"Yeah."

"I don't think so. These folks would've been mighty unhappy."

"I'm mighty unhappy."

"Sorry. Nothing I can do but refund your money."

"I don't want a refund. I want to toss a keg."

"Can't do it."

"So move everything out of the way, and we'll toss right here."

George could see what was coming, and he fervently hoped Ian had called security.

"I don't think so. We did what we could to let people know. We announced it on television, radio, Facebook, and our web page. We have contact information for people that signed up, and we called or sent emails or texts. You say you paid. Didn't you hear from us?"

"Let's just say I didn't. I wanna toss a keg."

"Don't have a keg for you to toss, buddy, or a place you can toss it."

"Well then, guess I'll have to toss you."

It happened so fast, George didn't actually register that he had been picked up until he found himself twirling in the air outside the tent. He landed on his back on the sand.

Then George was picked up by another man in the group, hoisted over his head, twirled and tossed. Once again, he landed on his back.

When the third man picked him up, George heard the first two arguing about who had the longest toss. "Mine went further than yours." "Only because he bounced."

Before he was thrown the third time, several security personnel tackled the man that held him. The man and George went down. Ian continued to click away.

Ian came in for a close-up. "Tell me you called them, Ian. Tell me you asked security to come."

"Someone else must have called. I was busy. Hey, are you hurt, buddy? Need an ambulance?"

George groaned and lay back on the sand, doing a mental check, head to toe, to assess potential damage.

He barely heard Ian say, "I'm gonna download these, too. Might need 'em."

Jennifer and Marie were stationed at the OktoberFest. They kept the ambulance near the beer tent. From experience, they knew this to be the location to receive most of the calls.

Jennifer picked up the radio when security gave a shout. "We're here. What is it and where is it?"

The voice on the radio had some static. Jennifer thought she heard "raid you and." "Say again?"

Marie walked over to listen. She heard, "Parade you and." "I think he means parade review stand."

"Really? Well, maybe someone got sick of seeing all those floats."

"Or hearing those bands. Golly. It was long this year."

Jennifer was already in the driver's seat. She started the ambulance and maneuvered it through crowds until she got to the review stand.

She and Marie stared at the stand. Then they stared at one another and started to laugh.

"Not again?!"

"They're gonna throw her in jail for sure this time!"

"I've got Annie."

"You got Annie last time."

"I called dibs."

"We don't have dibs in this business."

Jennifer jumped out of the truck, ready bag in hand, and sprinted to the review stand. She beat Marie to Annie by seconds.

"Next time, we're switching!"

Jennifer knelt beside Annie's chair. Annie held her head with one hand and curled the fingers of her other hand in and out, in and out.

"What happened?"

"I think he was going for my nose, but he got my head."

"He had pretty bad aim. Your hand's okay, though. You must have been holding something."

"My water bottle. An aluminum one."

"Good girl. You might put some ice on it when you get home, like you did last time, but this isn't nearly as bad as it was then."

Behind her, Jennifer heard Dan Tapper. In a high-pitched voice, he said, "Chee bwoke my node again! Chee bwoke my node!"

Marie was saying, "Calm down, Mr. Tapper. I have to take a look. There, that's good. Are you allergic to anything?"

Jennifer concentrated on Annie, looking carefully at her eyes. "You might have a minor concussion, Annie. I don't think you need to go to the hospital, but I want someone to watch you for the rest of the day. Should I call Chris or Henrie?"

"Chris is working. I don't know if Henrie has his phone. I don't think he's at the Inn right now."

"I'll try him." Jennifer tried his cellphone and waited. After five rings, Henrie answered. He sounded tired.

"Henrie, this is Jennifer. I'm sorry to bother you."

"Do not be concerned, Jennifer. How may I help you?"

"Well, there's been a little incident at the parade review stand."

"No."

"Yes."

"Is she hurt?"

"She may have a slight concussion. I don't think she needs to go to the hospital, but I don't want her to be alone."

"I am on my way. I will bring the golf cart. Tell me, did she, how shall I say this...defend herself?"

"Oh, yeah. I think she got him better this time."

"I am happy to hear it. I will be there shortly."

The radio sparked to life again. "What is it this time?"

"You need to ... beer tent."

"How bad is it?"

"One...sand...toss...egg."

"What?"

Marie called over her shoulder, "One man in the sand, tossed like a keg."

"You understood that?"

"Nope. I'm lookin' at it. It's George. He's on the ground."

Annie dropped her head into her hands as Jennifer picked up her bag. "You're going to be fine. I'll check on George."

Henrie had just settled Annie in the all-season porch with a pillow, blanket and cup of hot tea and a pile of cats. He left for the kitchen, saying over his shoulder, "You must eat something. I will prepare a small plate."

As soon as he reached the kitchen, the telephone rang. "KaliKo Inn. How may I help you?"

A male voice was on the other end. "Let me talk to Annie."

"She is indisposed. May I provide assistance?"

"I need to talk to her. Put her on."

"I am afraid that is not possible, sir. If I cannot assist you, perhaps I can take a message?"

"Are you in charge when she is...indisposed?"

"Yes, I believe you could say that."

"Well then you'd better figure out how you're going to come up with half a million dollars by Monday afternoon. I'm at least giving you time for the banks to open. Stay by the phone. All afternoon. Until I call with instructions. Oh. Before I forget, don't call the police."

Henrie, nearly always in control of his faculties, asked, "Is there a reason we would pay the sum you ask?"

"You're gonna pay, or you're not gonna see Mem again."

The caller disconnected.

Henrie stood for a moment, feelings of anger and scare alternately taking first place.

He disregarded the instructions he was given and called Pete.

Pete knew the caller, whom he supposed to be Dennis, or this person named Cooper, could have eyes on the street. He, Marco and Cyril left the police station and crossed the street to the Café. They turned left, as if walking south on Main Street, then turned into the back alley. From there, they broke into a trot and entered the grounds of the Inn from the back.

They continued to stay to the back, walking around the Inn and entering through the all-season porch door.

Henrie and Annie waited. Pete noticed the cats huddled behind chairs and sofas on the porch.

"Tell me everything about that call, Henrie."

"First, Pete, please tell us. Is Mem missing?"

"She is. I got the call about the time the parade ended, so not that long ago. You might want to know, Annie, that your cats have already given me a clue. But I don't want to tell you about it until you've told me everything you remember, Henrie."

Out of the corner of his eye, Pete saw Marco's face turn to a mask of confusion. Oops. He shouldn't have mentioned the cats in front of Marco.

Henrie relayed the information to Pete for a second time.

"What can you tell me about his voice?"

"Obviously male, I believe white, he sounded like an adult. While not polite, his diction and grammar were adequate until the end of the call. At that time, he used a familiar informal contraction on two occasions."

Inwardly, Pete both praised Henrie's gift for recall and grimaced at how he must sound, at times, to this very formal man.

"Could you detect an accent?"

"I would say midwestern."

"Could you hear anything in the background?"

Henrie considered the question. "Nothing that I could distinguish."

"Marco and I had just discussed looking at the video here. Is it okay if he goes to take a look?"

"Please, help yourself Marco. And help yourself to a cup of coffee while you are there."

"Thanks, Henrie." Marco nodded at Annie as he left. He turned back at the door. "Annie, I hear you got him again. I'm not supposed to say something like this, especially in front of my boss. You've got a career as a fighter!" Marco left the room. Kali, Ko and Mo followed at a discrete distance.

Annie looked at Pete. "How did he know about that? It just happened."

"Dan Tapper called. He wanted me to arrest you."

"Really? He started it."

"I figured he did. Anyway, investigating that nonsense thing is pretty far down on my list right now. Did you hear what I did?"

"You mentioned the cats in front of Marco."

Pete looked at the floor and shook his head. "It'll take a while for that to go out of his head. Anyway, this is what Tiger Lily did."

Tiger Lily jumped to Annie's side on the sofa while Pete dug into his shirt pocket for the pieces of paper. He opened them, smoothed them out and handed them to Annie.

She studied them while stroking Tiger Lily's back. "Dennis? Is that what this says?"

Cyril barked once. Tiger Lily purred.

"And this says 'Cooper'?"

Another bark. Another purr.

"So it might have been Dennis on the phone?"

"Adult male, white, midwestern accent. Could be him. I didn't want to pre-dispose you, Henrie."

"I doubt I could be predisposed in my recollections, but at least you can say that if it were to come up in a trial situation."

Pete gave Henrie half a smile.

"Marco remembered a former con that lives at that decrepit marina, so Cyril and I went out there. Cyril smelled Mem, so I know she is or was there. There's nothing I can do, legally, to get in there. I don't think Dennis will hurt her, so we've got some time. I need to build a case that is better than a note written by a cat and a dog's nose. Now that he's asked for money, I'll be able to come up with something."

"Speaking of money, there's no way I can come up with half a million dollars. We had this situation when the cats were kidnapped. I couldn't come up with less money then, and my situation is the same now."

"No one would expect you to, Annie. You are the point of contact, and we need to work with that. For now, you need to go on as if nothing happened. Marco and I will do what we have to do, call in who we have to call in, and…well…we're going to have to be here, somehow, behind the scenes on Monday afternoon. Set up what the TV folks would call a 'command station.' We might have to come up with a way to get the money. Just in case. But it won't be from you, Annie. And I'll have to come up with an excuse to have officers stationed at that marina."

Pete joined Marco in the kitchen, grabbing a cup of coffee in the process. He pulled a chair up behind Marco and looked at the screens. The time stamp was six thirty in the morning. "What time did you go back to?"

"Diana said Mem stayed overnight at Frank's and left about seven, so I backed up to five, in case someone was waiting on the street. So far, I haven't seen anyone that I don't know or know of. And I haven't seen Dennis."

"I'll bet he took her when she left Frank's. Darn the luck. No cameras there until next week."

They watched until they saw Diana leave the yoga studio with Harrison. Nothing popped up as suspicious.

Cyril chatted quietly with Tiger Lily as they listened to Pete talk. *"I smelled her. She's in one of those old trailers. I wanted to go in, but I know Pete has rules."*

"But you're sure she's there? Is there anything we can do?"

"Not now. We have to keep our eyes open for a legitimate reason to go in. Pete seems to think that since a ransom has been requested, he might be able to come up with an excuse. I'm not sure what it would be."

"We'll keep an eye out. Did you hear what happened to Mommy?"

"I did. It's good to see she's okay, but that idiot wants Pete to arrest her."

"We were all sitting on the porch about the time it happened, but then you and Pete ran up The Avenue because of Mem…and we were distracted. We left her all alone, and she needed us."

"It seems to me she took care of herself without anyone's help. That's the way to do it!"

24

Activity in the park and on the beach cooled down while The Avenue heated up.

George, relieved from clean-up duty, but already scheduled off from Mo's Tap, sat with Candice, Ian and Anna in the garden behind the Winery and Mo's. He looked around, thinking, so this is what it's like to come out on a Saturday date night.

Hannah and Eve sat at a table, gazing with starry eyes at the band. It appeared to George that they looked at the drummer, Manny. Trudie sat at a two-top with the high school teacher that Candice used to date. She had eyes only for him.

George looked at the band, wondering what had happened to her fascination with Manny. Manny ignored everyone else in the room. When he looked at the crowd, he looked at Trudie. He was looking at her now. George turned back. Trudie had eyes only for the teacher.

Poor schmuck, thought George. He's being used. Before the weekend is over, Manny will be coming after Trudie, which is exactly what she wants. Women!

The band played jazz, but tonight they had dipped into their blues repertoire. They played a jazzy version of BB King's Three O'Clock Blues. George took a deep breath and unconsciously touched his bandaged midsection. Three cracked ribs and a pulled muscle in his left upper arm. Not bad for two and a half tosses.

He continued his gaze across the room. Emme had gone young. She was at a table with Boone's older son, Daryl. He was probably in his early twenties to her, what, mid-thirties? There was a cougar in town. And she wrote romance novels.

He didn't see Nan. George looked at Anna. "Where's Nan? I see everyone else from your group."

"She's at the Inn writing. There's been so much good material for her mystery novels. She wanted to get on it while it was fresh in her mind."

The conversation between Ian, Anna and Candice floated around in the background of his thoughts. The pain pills didn't help.

He worried about Diana, a friend from childhood. As far as he knew, there was no word yet of where her mother was or with whom. Diana seemed to think Mem might be with Dennis, and against her will.

James was still in the hospital, still in an induced coma. Ginger had taken the younger children, Ava and Carl, to the home of her parents. Laila packed a bag and stayed in the hospital room with James. George couldn't help but shake his head. No mother should have to go through this. And Laila was going through it a second time with James. He had been roughed up protecting his friend Ginger just a few months ago.

Annie had decked that reporter again. George smiled to himself as he remembered the evening news. The anchor announced, without any inflection, that Dan Tapper would be on vacation for "an undetermined period of time." He couldn't wait to see what Juanita from the morning newspaper had to say.

And he hoped Annie was okay.

Ian was saying something. "…and then this guy just picks him up, carries him outside the tent, twirls around holding him over his head, and tosses him…" George gave a benign smile as Ian shared the pictures.

In the front corner, Clara sat with Pete and Janet, and Ray and Cheryl. They had come to visit with Ramon, and to hear him play, but more than that, they brought their companions. Fiamma, Cyril and Jock were around the corner in the tasting room, a bit away from the sound of the music, alternately looking at one another and napping. A time or two, one dog or another would ask to be let out, and all three would – no doubt – take a walk along The Avenue, enjoying the crisp, fall evening. He saw the little Jack Russel Terrier, too. Tillie was in and out. She seemed to take messages from the dogs and bring messages back….George stopped himself. He leaned in and said, "Candice, I have to go. The pain, the pills, a glass of wine – that I shouldn't have had – and…I'm just not thinking straight."

"Go on. I'll be up pretty soon."

As George walked out through Mo's, he noticed Geraldine and her husband, Everett, at a table. So they were still together. Perhaps Geraldine didn't like to look at a face with a busted nose.

Henrie, Annie and Chris sat on the all-season porch. Annie drank iced tea while Chris had wine. Henrie had something that looked like bourbon. Annie noticed his drawn face and – unusual for him – downturned mouth. At first, she thought Mem's situation was the cause. Then she remembered her conversation with Ian.

"Henrie, I hate to bring this up, because you look so tired this evening, but…well…I heard something that you should know."

Henrie sat up straighter and looked at her. "Yes?"

"Ian wanted to talk to you today. It isn't as if he was talking around you. You weren't there, and, well, he was concerned."

"What was his concern?"

"He said that last night, when he had dinner with Anna, she told him about a woman that was at Mo's asking questions about you Thursday night. When he described the woman, I realized I had seen her, but she wasn't asking questions when I was there."

Henrie looked at his drink and said nothing. Chris watched their faces and kept his thoughts to himself.

"Anyway, I saw her, and I would recognize her if we looked at the videos." Annie paused for a few seconds. Henrie still looked at his drink. Chris still held his tongue. "Do you want to look for her? See if you recognize her?"

Henrie finally spoke, but he didn't look up. "There is no need. I saw her yesterday, when I tried to figure out how to work the controls to the monitor. I know her."

"Who is she?"

"Apparently, she is not the woman I thought she was."

They sat in silence for several minutes. Chris finally found his tongue. "Henrie, you are the most private person I have ever known. But you have to know you have friends here. Two of your best friends are sitting right here in this room. Will you let us in? Let us help you?"

"Chris...I...well...you see, I thought..." Henrie's eyes roamed the room. His head turned this way and that, looking mostly at the floor or the ceiling, never at Chris and Annie.

He started again. "I met her – Cassandra – some time ago. I was in Marsh Haven, shopping, and she was just...there...and we began to talk. At the time, I wondered why someone like her would be shopping in the same place as I. Silly, I suppose, but when thinking about it today, that came to mind again. I wonder now if perhaps she had arranged to meet me. If she had followed me. But I have no earthly reason to think that."

Annie remained silent, happy for Chris to be with them and carry the ball. He did. "Did you come up with any reason she might want to meet you?"

"No. She has asked often about the town, the Inn, the other places here on The Avenue, about you, Annie. But those questions seemed to come in the normal conversation of two people getting to know one another."

"What did you learn about her?"

"I have not been there, but she relayed to me that she owns a fine dining establishment in the city, one that specializes in Mediterranean and Egyptian cuisine. As a matter of fact, she has used that restaurant as an excuse to not be able to be away for more than one day or one evening at a time."

"You've invited her to come here?"

"Often. As a matter of fact, I had finally come to the opinion that if I want a relationship – a long term relationship – that I would have to move to the city. This is something I might have discussed with you next week,

Annie, the possibility of it, and what your next steps might be, but now…now…there is no consideration. I would not be able to, as it were, continue in any type of a relationship with someone who withholds…well, I'm not sure what she is withholding…."

The three remained silent while they considered Henrie's dilemma and watched the moon rise. Finally, Annie said, "Have you ever considered Googling her to see what comes up?"

"Googling?"

Coming from Henrie's mouth, Annie had to laugh, but she stifled it. "Yes. Do you know her full name?"

"I have a full name. As I considered it today, my question is, do I have a correct name."

"And the name of the restaurant?"

"Yes. I have not investigated the restaurant, but I know the name."

"There is no time like the present. Let's go to the kitchen and take a look."

They sat at the computer, going through Google and looking, occasionally, at the monitors to see how the cameras worked in real time. It was research. Really! Annie didn't even laugh when she saw Geraldine and her husband together again.

As they went up to Annie's apartment, Chris asked, "Did you notice the cats tonight?"

"No. What were they doing?"

"They were in and out of the porch when we were there, and Tillie was in and out. If I were a betting man –

you know I'm not – I would bet Tillie and those cats were up to something. I don't know what."

"Don't be silly. They were just playing. Tillie gets lonely all by herself."

Cyril, Jock and Fiamma had come to a comfortable part of their friendship. Fiamma didn't flirt with them – at least not too much – and they reigned in their jealousy of one another in her presence.

Fiamma had leapt up in joy when they both entered the Winery. *"I've missed you!"*

The boys were so exuberant in their greeting that Ray had finally said, "Outside! All of you! I'll come get you in a few minutes. Run it off."

And they had. They ran up and down The Avenue with abandon. They called at the window for Tillie to come down and play. She had, and she went in and out of the winery with them for the rest of the evening.

Mostly, she carried messages to and from the dogs and the cats. She could get through the cat doors. The big dogs were hampered in that regard.

Before the evening was over, the dogs and the cats knew everything that had happened and were ready to help their humans if and when the opportunity arose. Mem's kidnapping was still on top of their list, but everyone was amazed that Henrie had a girlfriend and that she was a meany.

25

Annie sat in the back pew and held her hand to her temple. She still had a bit of a headache. She was glad she and Henrie had been excused from clean-up detail at the OktoberFest.

The cats were very helpful. They understood she was in pain, and they took turns sitting in her lap, pushing up against her left hip or her right, climbing onto her shoulder…very helpful. Even the new little boy kitty snuggled close.

Pastor Teresa had a lengthy announcements portion during the church service. Annie listened with half an ear.

"Until further notice, we need some help taking care of Ava and Carl. Ginger has permission to miss her classes this week and will work at the store, which means she can't watch the kids."

Annie made a mental note to invite them to the Inn for a day. Not today.

"Also, you all know that Mem is missing. It is presumed that this is not of her choosing. If there is anyone who knows anything or hears anything, even if you think it's useless information, please call Pete."

Annie was amazed word of the ransom call had not leaked.

"A couple of our prime volunteers sustained some injuries yesterday, so we're looking for extra folks to help clean up the park and the beach after church. I think that's all, unless someone has something else to add?"

For once, the community potluck at the private beach was canceled. Annie and Henrie walked home together, some cats in front and some behind. They entered the Inn to sounds they would not miss at all in the coming days.

"Hurry UP! We have to get on the ROAD!"

Six cats rushed to get under the detective table. Two rushed back to Henrie's apartment.

"The CAR is already PACKED! WHAT's the RUSH?"

"HANNAH, don't FORGET! Give HENRIE his COFFEE cup!"

"Did you pack LEFTOVERS? That BREAKFAST was DIVINE!"

"I'm going to MISS THAT the MOST."

"I'm going to miss IAN."

"JUST BECAUSE you found a MAN before WE did…"

Henrie walked into the kitchen. Annie followed. Chris sat at the table, cup of coffee in hand. "This is the first time I've heard it. This is what you've been living with?"

"Pretty much." Annie leaned over to kiss the top of his head. And she looked at the newspaper on the table in front of him. "What the…"

"They must have paid Ian for a good picture."

Annie picked it up. The front page, on top of the fold, held a full color photograph of the connecting crunch. Annie's face showed both anger and scare. It was amazing the photograph didn't show a red and green aura around her body.

"I'll bet that aluminum thing packed a wallop. It looks like a straight-on shot. I forgot to ask if you'd called your attorney."

Just then, the telephone rang. Annie handed the newspaper to Henrie and picked up the phone. "Well, good morning, Jenny. We were just talking about you."

"Do you have more pictures? Before and after?"

"Yes. Ian said his camera was set to burst, whatever that means, and just to be safe, he copied them to George's computer."

"Good. Come in tomorrow and bring me a copy. They're going to sue. Or they say they're going to sue. Let's convince them not to do that."

"Alright. Is nine o'clock good for you?"

"Sure. See you then."

Annie hung up. "I love it when people you care for take care of you." She looked at Henrie. With a bit of a point.

No one got another word out before they heard, "We're LEAVING!" "THANK YOU!" "See you NEXT year!"

"Do you think we need to answer them?"

Henrie listened. "No. They are gone."

"Do you think we can be full before they call next year?"

"Not a chance. They have booked. I tried to make it painful by requiring a fifty percent nonrefundable deposit, due to the year in advance."

The cats started to drift into the kitchen, looking from side to side, just to be sure one of the women wasn't lurking behind an appliance.

"And they paid it?"

"Unfortunately."

"And the band? Have they had breakfast?"

"I took a bountiful supply of items to the carriage house. It is my understanding that BeeBop and Manny will cook for them all. Probably early this afternoon."

Henrie gathered items for lunch, and Chris brought up the subject that Henrie didn't want to discuss. "What do we do with the things we learned last night?"

Henrie looked down. Kali and Ko circled his ankles, rubbing against him, leaving their love hairs on his pants, seeming to know that he might not like the conversation.

"Which lie do we tackle first? The one about the restaurant, or the one about being a native of the city?"

"Or how about what she would be looking for when she engineered a meeting with you, Henrie? She's been stalking you as a potential employee."

Their foray into Google the night before led to the discovery that yes, there was a high-end restaurant specializing in Mediterranean and Egyptian cuisine, but it was inside a high-end hotel, one of several in a chain that stretched from Chicago to New York. The name of the owner, Cassandra Laurent, led to links with the owners of Henrie's former employers.

"I have considered this. However, one must not make assumptions hastily. Linking her interest with me with knowledge of my previous employer seems to be reasonable. However, why would an owner of such a massive company run personal research of this nature?"

"Remember, she is only recently the owner. She was a daughter. Now she's at the top of the heap. Maybe she's looking to put her personal stamp on the corporation."

Chris added, "Maybe she wants to branch out. Maybe Henrie is only part of it. Maybe she wants what you own, Annie."

"What?"

"Think about it. She came here. She did not want to meet you before coming here. She engineered being in at least two of your places to…I don't know…check them out?"

"Let's back up and think that it's Henrie she's after. Is this something you want?"

"The money would be gratifying. The responsibilities would provide an adequate challenge. But even before I know the location or locations she might have in mind for me, I can say – and this is unqualified – no. I do not want it. Not now. Not ever. This life, this place, these people, are home to me now."

"But you were considering moving to the city."

"That was…well…when I thought something more would come with it. When I thought…"

Annie said, "Love is hard."

Chris, almost under his breath, said, "Yes. It is."

Annie threw a jab at Chris's upper arm for that comment. Then she looked back at Henrie. "Do you think she'll ask you, Henrie? Ask you to go to work for her? Or ask to see you again?"

"I do not know. I do not intend to call her. She will have to make the first move. And there will never, under any circumstance, be the pretense of a personal relationship with her again."

Chris nursed his upper arm and shook his head. "Henrie, I'm sorry. Really sorry."

Just then, they heard a tentative voice from the foyer. "Hello? Is anybody here?"

Henrie rose to greet whoever it was. Annie followed and watched from the dining room door.

"How may I help you?"

"You the folks got all the cats?"

"Certainly, cats live here, yes."

"Well, we heard you had cats here, and sometimes cats that are lost or strayed or somethin', sometimes they come here?"

Leaning against the dining room door, Annie felt a cat against her ankles. She looked down. It was the new kitty.

"That has happened on occasion, yes."

"Well, we been worried about a cat. He lived at the state park, ya know, and the guy that had 'im, well, he was the one killed."

The little cat walked into the foyer tentatively. The man saw him.

"Daryll? Is that you, Daryll?"

The cat ran to the man and allowed himself to be picked up. He purred and clung to the man's shoulder.

"I'm so glad I found you, feller. We been worried about you, and that's a fact."

Daryll purred some more.

Annie moved into the room. "I'm Annie, this is Henrie. And you are?"

"Oh, yes ma'am. I'm Fred. I work at the park. Well, we was awful worried about Daryll. We was talkin', an' I said I'd see if he come here. You know. We been puttin' food out an' all, but he never come to eat. I'm real happy you got 'im. Real happy."

"He's been really sweet. I didn't know…"

"Well, there was no way you coulda known. I'll be happy to tell 'em that Daryll has a good home."

Annie and Henrie looked at one another, then back at Fred. "You don't want to take him? Back to the park?"

"It wouldn't be safe for 'im to live alone in the park, ma'am. And we, none of us, can take the little feller. None of us owns our homes, you see, and we can't have pets. None of us. We've asked ever'body."

"I see. Well you don't have to worry. Daryll can stay here until we find a home for him."

"Really? You'll do that fer 'im?"

"Yes. You know, Daryll seems to like you a lot. Are you sure you don't want to take him?"

"I like him too, ma'am, but like I say, I can't keep 'im. An' without someone to take care of 'im all the time, well, the park just ain't that safe for a little cat."

Annie moved closer and put her head close to Daryll. Softly, she said, "So you're Daryll, huh? And you've had a very bad week. I'm so glad you found your way here."

Daryll purred some more, and he lifted his head to look at Annie. Annie held out her hands for him and he loosed his grip on Fred's shoulder. Annie took him. He latched onto hers.

"He seems to understand that you can't keep him, Fred. We'll keep him safe and healthy here, and we'll find a good home for him."

"Well, thanky, ma'am. I'm gonna tell ever'one about this. They'll be so happy. Daryll, I'm real glad I found you. I'll tell ever'one you're safe. And, ya know, I'm real sorry about, well, you know."

Daryll buried his head in Annie's neck.

"Thank you, Fred. Thank you very much."

"Yes'um." Fred nodded at Henrie and backed out the door.

"So, Daryll. That's your name. We'll find a good home for you. And you're welcome here until then. For as long as it takes."

Tiger Lily and Chris had entered the foyer at some point. Annie didn't know when. Tiger Lily gave Annie a look that said, "I found him. I get to keep him."

Annie was saved an argument with the cats, because Pete walked in. Behind him were Frank, Diana and Harrison.

Annie approached both Diana and Frank with a hug.

Harrison looked around. "It's as pretty as I remember. Annie, we're here to talk about the, um, thing. Is there anyone in the house that shouldn't hear?"

Annie asked, "Henrie, do you think Jules and Noelle are still upstairs?"

"It is possible. Allow me to make an investigatory trip."

Henrie left the Inn. Through the windows, Harrison watched as Henrie walked through the yard to the carriage house. He looked at Annie in confusion.

241

"Jules and Noelle are connected to the folks in the carriage house, the band. They were going to cook breakfast over there today. Brunch. Lunch with breakfast food. Something."

Henrie returned. "I am happy to report they have everything they need, and everyone is present and accounted for in the carriage house. No one is in the Inn."

With so many people, cats and a big dog, they settled in the library. Harrison was in control of this gathering, and he wasted no time getting down to it. "I have the money, Annie. It will arrive by messenger no later than ten o'clock tomorrow morning. He will appear to be a guest of the Inn, and he'll bring in several suitcases, all things the police will need here. He's a member of my private security team. If we reach a point that the money must be delivered, he will take on that responsibility."

"We'll be ready for him. Does he need a room, too? In case this takes more than one day?"

"If you have a room available, that will help seal it. Just in case anyone comes in, we want him to look like he belongs here."

Annie and Henrie nodded.

"Where will you set up, Pete, and how will you get in here without being seen?"

"Marco is working with the state police. A few of their experts will be here, and they'll get in the same way we did yesterday. They'll either walk the back way from the marina, or they'll come down the alley from Main Street. They'll come in ones and twos."

Pete thought for a minute. He looked at Henrie. "Do you have a place we can go, so if someone comes in off the street they won't see a crowd of people and equipment?"

Annie was the one to answer. "My apartment. It's the only place. No one would look there."

She turned to Henrie. "You'd better call Hilly and give her some excuse. Tell her I'm coming down with something and I don't want to share. You and I can clean the rooms tomorrow."

Harrison reached over to take Diana's hand. "It will be okay, Diana. She'll be home tomorrow."

Pete's radio crackled to life. "Pete, the hospital called. That boy is awake. He's okay, and he can talk to you now."

Bergamasco took advantage of the empty private beach. They packed their brunch and walked around the back of the Inn, not bothering anyone inside. They carried chillers with white wine and wine coolers, coolers of artisan beer, hampers of fried chicken and potato salad, and all of the items Henrie had laid in for them.

Clara had called Felicity and Trudie to join them. Trudie asked if she could bring a guest. Her date from the night before was with her. Clara smiled to herself and looked surreptitiously at Manny when she announced the women were on the way. "Trudie's bringing her friend."

Manny had looked down quickly, masking whatever emotion he felt.

Clara kept an eye on the situation throughout the afternoon. Trudie was a master. Without appearing to rub it into Manny's face, she made a perfectly wonderful display of being friendly to everyone but interested only in the teacher. The poor guy, thought Clara. If he only knew how much he was being used.

Fiamma was painfully lonely. She had finally seen her handsome big boys, Cyril and Jock, the night before. The boys made her visits to Chelsea satisfying. She'd heard people talking about the moonlight cruise on Friday, and on Saturday, she heard snippets about the crimes, which she thought would keep Cyril busy. But no. He and his humans had come to the Winery, along with Jock and his humans. Today, though, she was all by herself.

Until she heard the cats. The cats, bless them, had come to join her on the beach. She wouldn't have to be alone after all! She ran, rolled in the sand, dug holes, watched them fil up with water. Swam in the shallow part of the lake, and rolled in the sand some more. It was a glorious day!

Every now and then, Fiamma glanced back at a new kitty. Tiger Lily stayed with him. He seemed just a bit sad. Lonely. Scared. He'd be okay. He had a new family, and they would take care of him.

26

Billy didn't like the county jail. He'd been here before, but in the juvenile section. This place was bad. Real bad.

He and his crew had been separated. Billy heard – through the jail grapevine – that Justin bonded out. Too bad. He wanted a shot at Billy. Because of him, his right arm was in a cast. Fractured bone. No wonder it hurt.

He couldn't stop thinking about Justin. Rich kid. That's what he was. He wasn't cut out for the life. He was probably singing his little heart out. Had to be. He probably got his charges lowered, too. They'd all come in on the same counts, and he, Billy, couldn't bond out. Not yet, anyway.

Billy thought about his situation. Several counts of malicious trespass. Felony assault. Felony assault with intent to kill. And that cop was saying that he could still be charged with murder.

If that nerd kid doesn't wake up and tell them the body was there first, they're going to pin that murder on me. On me!

Billy wasn't the cock of the walk in the county jail. He was more like Porter. When he got here, he tried to act tough, but after taking a couple of beatings, well, he was just going to have to pretend to be invisible.

Maybe there's something I can give them, he thought. Just maybe.

Billy approached the bars. "You! Hey you! Tell that cop that arrested me I got somethin' to say!"

Pete stood and Laila sat by the bed in the intensive care unit. James clung to her hand. Pete had promised the doctor he would go easy on James, let him go at his own pace.

"We'll go slow, James. For now, just tell me what you remember, and if I have any questions, I'll ask. But we won't do too much today."

"Okay. Well, I was in that grove of trees, the ones on the lake side of the community building. I was watching for the bullies, and they came. Just like I thought. They broke a window or something. I heard a crack and then I heard glass break."

"You stayed in the trees?"

"Yeah. I was calling nine-one-one, and I was walking backwards. I wanted to get a little further away, so they wouldn't hear me. And then I tripped. I landed on the ground, and I think my head hit something, because I remember waking up. I don't know how long I was out."

James got silent.

"Do you need to rest?"

"No. I was just thinking. When I woke up, I remembered I tripped over something. I found my phone, and I picked it up. I used the flashlight app, and then I saw the body. I started screaming, and, well, I might have done that for a while."

Pete gave it a few seconds. He said, "And then?"

"And then I got hit over the head."

"Are you sure the body was there before you saw the boys?"

"Yeah. Apparently, I'd been sitting really close to it for a long time, and then the bullies came, and then I found it."

"Okay. For now, that's all I need to hear, James. You do everything the doctors tell you to do, okay?"

"Yes, sir. And I'm really sorry, Pete."

"For what?"

"For being so stupid, and for trying to convince Ginger to join me."

Pete's phone vibrated in his pocket. He excused himself and answered. Pete walked into the hall to listen. His dispatcher said, "That boy, Billy, at the county jail, he says he's got something you want to hear."

"Any indication what it is?"

"No. He just told the guards you'd want to know it quick."

"Alright. Tell them I'm on my way."

Pete got to the car and let Cyril out for a walk. "Sorry. We're going to the jail next, and you can't go in there, either."

Cyril huffed, but took a walk and took care of some business.

On the road, Pete talked through the situations at hand with Cyril. This helped him get things straight in his mind. And recently, he'd come to know that it was a good thing for Cyril to have all the information that he had. Because Cyril had a way of putting two and two together.

At the jail, Pete cracked a window for Cyril before going in. When Billy was shown into the interview room, Pete said, "This had better be good. I've had a very long day, and I won't be happy to have come this far for nothing."

"Oh, I got something. But I want a deal."

"What kind of deal?"

"Most of the charges gone. A malicious trespass. Nothing else."

"Do you want an attorney now?"

"No."

"Let me repeat your rights." Pete read Billy his rights again and Billy assured him that he understood them.

"Okay. Now you have to tell me the nature of this information, so I know if it's something worth my while. And, you have to know the district attorney would have to agree to drop or change anything, now that charges have been filed."

"You'll deal with me. You're lookin' for a woman. I may know where she is."

Annie was asleep. The cats gathered on the windowsill looking over The Avenue. Tiger Lily said, *"Tomorrow is going to be an important day. The police will be here, and they're going to send more police to get Mem."*

"Did we helps, Tiger Lily?"

"Yes, Sassy Pants. We helped a lot. We did everything we could do, and Cyril did the rest. They know where she is. They just have to make sure they can arrest the people who did it."

"I don't understand about this evidence stuff. Why couldn't Pete just go get her?"

"*I think he believes she's safe for now, at least until they get the money. And there is something about laws and things to — Cyril calls it to protect the innocent — anyway, there are laws. And he has to follow them, because he's a police officer.*"

"*But it doesn't make any sense.*"

"*I know. But think about it the other way around. What if someone accused Mommy of doing something bad, and without any proof, some police officer arrested her and took her away. We would be without a mommy and a home, and she'd be in jail, and there wouldn't be anything we could do about it.*"

"*But…*"

"*I know. It seems like a no-brainer. But it's not.*"

Mr. Bean started to laugh. He laughed so hard he nearly fell off the windowsill. When he finally got himself under control, he asked, "*How much sand do you think Fiamma had in her hair after the beach today?*"

This started a round of laughter from all of the cats, even Daryll, who had watched the fun from afar. Fiamma must have carried away three pounds of sand in that glorious, long, matted hair.

27

While the state police set up in her apartment, Annie served coffee and set out a platter of baked goods from Mr. Bean's. Because she didn't want to call attention to the Inn, the baked goods had been purchased in batches, one each by Diana, Frank and Pete. No one else knew what would go on in this building on this day.

Annie listened as closely as she could as Pete talked into a radio headset, coordinating some kind of stakeout. As it turned out, Pete didn't need to fabricate an excuse to have officers at the old marina. A statement from one of the bully boys provided him the evidence he needed.

She also fielded texts and calls about the cats and why they weren't at work. "I have the flu, and they all decided to stay home with me." More than once, she had to say, "I don't need anything. Really. Henrie is taking care of me."

Annie walked past Marco and a state trooper a few times while she filled coffee cups. She heard, "...pretty sure he was killed by mistake...thought he was Dennis?...saw too much?...must have bugged out...figure out who they are...find them...Pete must have ESP...asked me about a guy named Cooper...yeah, turns out...."

Annie sat in her reclining chair in the living room and in view of the activity in the dining room. Daryll jumped onto the arm of the chair, then tentatively put a paw in her lap. Annie relaxed and allowed him to think about it. Soon, he came to her lap and curled up.

Annie cupped his head with one hand and spoke softly. "You heard them, too, huh? Sounds like Mr. Stimson may have gotten killed by mistake. Or he may have just been in the wrong place at the wrong time. Either way, that's very sad. I'm very sorry you have to go through this."

Annie felt the little cat snuggle closer. After a few minutes, she felt a purr start, and soon, he was asleep. Annie fell asleep also.

She was worn out from several nights in a row with little sleep, worry, and work. She and Henrie had cleaned and reset the guest rooms – all but the carriage house and the one room still held by Jules and Noelle – before Annie was typically out of bed.

When they finished, Annie left dealing with guests to Henrie, and she set up the room for the police officers and technicians that started to arrive by mid-morning.

Henrie arranged for breakfast for members of the band at the Café, telling them that Annie was fairly contagious, and since they would be leaving today, he didn't want to take the chance of passing something on to them. They were happy to oblige. Jules promised to take their luggage to the carriage house as they left for breakfast.

All in all, Henrie had things well in hand. In an unusual move for the Inn, he locked the front door as soon as Jules and Noelle left.

Annie awoke to Pete's hand on her shoulder. "Annie, wake up. It's noon; you need to come in and wait with us."

Annie put the little cat on the floor as she stood up. She stretched, yawned, and shook herself awake. She knew the script. She knew the rules of the game. All she had to do now was put on a great act when Dennis – if it was Dennis – called.

The state police lead investigator, a slew of technicians, Harrison and Harrison's security man, Al, sat at the dining room table. They had the same build and similar hair and skin coloring. When they were introduced, Harrison had said, "He was chosen because sometimes he acts as my double."

Annie was told again, "When he tells you where to deliver the money, verify the address or the directions, and remember to tell him you can't bring it yourself. You received a concussion on Saturday and you've been told not to drive under any circumstances."

"And then I tell him that Harrison will drive my car."

"And when he asks you why Harrison knows about this?"

"I had to tell him. I couldn't get to the bank on my own this morning."

"And why didn't Henrie help you?"

"Are you kidding? A black man helping a woman get half a million out of the bank? That wouldn't work."

Harrison added, "If Diana's memories of him are on point, he'll accept that explanation without question."

Annie brought out her cell phone and played Farkle to keep herself awake. Then Klondike Solitaire. Then she read her CNN newsfeed, read the USA Today newsfeed, checked her email, looked at the weather, looked at her text messages, and read Facebook posts for as long as she could stand it. Shortly after starting the cycle again, and midway into her second game of Farkle, the telephone rang.

Everyone jumped to attention. Annie picked up on the second ring.

"Hello?"

"You got it?"

"Yes."

The voice on the other end of the line told her where to bring it. Several technicians wrote furiously.

"Please repeat the directions."

"You got it the first time."

"Okay, then please let me read them back to you."

A technician handed a sheet of paper to her and she repeated the directions.

"You got it. Leave in fifteen minutes."

"Alright, except it won't be me. It will be Harrison."

"What? I didn't give permission for that. It's got to be you. And why did you tell him?"

"I had to. I received a concussion Saturday, and I can't drive. When you called Saturday, I was at the hospital. I had to get help from someone."

"Why didn't you get that man to help? The one that answered the phone?"

"Are you kidding? If a black man drove me to the bank and helped me withdraw that kind of money, the police would have been called right away."

"Well…you're probably right. You could have told Diana. She could have helped."

"Certainly you realize the police are watching her. If she did something like that, they'd follow her."

"Oh. Okay. You give those directions to Harrison, then, and he's got fifteen minutes from now to leave."

Annie hung up and stopwatches were set.

Pete, from the corner of the room, said, "The man seemed to know both Harrison and Diana. It's got to be Dennis."

Pete turned away and got on the radio again. Annie heard him give instructions to someone on the other end.

Before she knew it, Al was on his way. She sat in a corner. Harrison joined her, and Henrie sat close.

They waited.

Annie was able to figure out what was happening without getting in the way or asking questions. Several units were on the waterfront. Some would follow Dennis, or whoever it was, and others would stay to look for Mem when he left. Still other units followed Al.

It didn't take long for voices to begin to whisper, then talk, then shout instructions over the various radios in the room. The man, they called him Dennis, was on the move. Someone found Mem. A man named Cooper was taken into custody. Mem was taken to an ambulance and nothing more was said about her. Once they knew Mem was safe, the order was given to take Dennis down.

Controlled pandemonium erupted. Annie could decipher some of it. Al stayed on target for the meeting place and stopped, staying in the car as he had been instructed. Some police officers had been dispatched as soon as directions had been given, and Al was in sight.

Then Dennis was spotted. They knew they had all the evidence they needed to arrest him, so there was no need to wait. Annie, Harrison and Henrie by her side, listened in real time as Dennis was taken into custody.

For Annie, the arrest was a bit…dull. No shouts, no gunfire, no cries of, "I'm innocent!" Only a loud voice telling Dennis to get out of the car, and a resigned voice that said, "Dag nab it."

While the officers and technicians around the table rejoiced in their success, Annie sat, tense and worried, waiting to hear about Mem. Finally, she could take it no longer. Her voice trembled as she asked, "Is Mem alright?"

Pete, still in the dining room, said, "I'm sorry, Annie, I should have told you. Mem's fine. She's hungry, thirsty and tired. She's on her way to the hospital to be checked out."

Harrison, tense as a wire, asked, "Can I leave now? I have to tell Diana. Tell Frank. Can we go to the hospital?"

"Sure. We'll need you to come by and make a statement later today."

Harrison looked at Annie, nearly panicked. She read his mind. He didn't know what to do first. She said, "Get Diana. I'll call Frank. He'll meet you at the hospital."

Harrison nearly ran out of the apartment and down the stairs.

Annie looked at Henrie. They both took a deep breath.

Henrie asked, "Back to normal?"

"Back to normal. I'll call Frank then send out a text blast to let everyone know."

Annie didn't notice the collective sigh from the living room. The large pile of cats and a big dog left their long vigil in search of food and water.

Henrie sat in his favorite chair, feet up, a shot of bourbon neat on the end table, satisfied with the day's ending. The Inn's telephone rang. He picked up the handheld.

"KaliKo Inn, how may I help you?"

The voice on the other end of the line was lush. "I've decided I'm ready for you to tell Annie about me. May I come over?"

Henrie looked at the clock. "It is late, and I have had a long day. I would prefer not, at this time."

"I know it's late, but perhaps I can come over, and you can introduce me to Annie in the morning?"

Henrie didn't know quite what to say. "This is not a good time. It would take you more than an hour to drive here, and truly, the day has been quite eventful. I am not up to seeing you."

"Well, that's too bad, because I'm parked in your driveway."

Henrie sighed audibly.

"Is there a problem, Henrie?"

"The short answer is 'yes.'"

"Well, no better time to deal with it than the present, don't you think?"

"You are absolutely correct. Please give me a few minutes, then come to the front door."

Henrie sent Annie a text, took a drink, checked to see that Annie had received the text, and walked slowly to the foyer.

When he opened the door, there she was. Cassandra. On a Monday night, she was dressed in a short, tight, low-cut black dress. Small diamonds sparkled in her ears, and a diamond teardrop necklace offset her coffee-colored skin. She was posed, hip against the door jamb, right arm as high as it could reach, right hand curled around the jamb. Her face curved into her arm.

Annie reached the first floor in time to see her in that pose, Chris at her heels. Eight cats came to a screeching halt at the bottom of the steps, backs arched, fur extended and claws at the ready. Kali and Ko walked on stiff legs to stand beside Henrie. Low hisses came from both of them.

Cassandra disengaged from her pose. She looked down and said, "These big girls must be Kali and Ko. How precious."

They hissed again.

Tiger Lily took charge of the felines. Assuming this would be a formal conversation, she ordered the cats to go into the library. When Kali and Ko didn't comply immediately, she nudged each with her shoulder until they turned to go. They stalked into the library but continued to look over their shoulders at the offending woman.

"Aren't you going to invite me in?"

"Please," said Henrie, "come in. May I introduce you, Cassandra, to Annie, and this is Chris."

"Charmed, I'm sure. I was not prepared to meet you tonight, Annie. I thought perhaps I would meet you later? In the morning? But tonight is good, too."

Annie said, "Henrie, why don't you show your guest into the library. Chris and I will bring out drinks." She looked at Cassandra. "Coffee or tea? Perhaps wine or something stronger?"

"I like a good martini. Vodka. Top shelf."

"Not a problem." Annie and Chris left. Henrie knew that Chris was the necessary ingredient. Annie couldn't make a good martini if her life depended on it. He doubted she would know a top shelf vodka from a bar well gin.

"Come this way, Cassandra."

As they seated themselves, Henrie asked, "This seems a bit impetuous for you. Typically, our meetings are planned in advance."

"I confess I wanted to see for myself that you were…single…in this house."

"Perhaps the level of trust that we have with one another is not up to standard."

"Henrie, I trust you implicitly. I just…wanted to make sure."

Henrie sat, looked at Cassandra and waited several seconds. He needed to wait until Annie and Chris returned before confronting her.

"Forgive me if I do not seem to be in the best of moods. As I said before, the day was quite eventful."

"Why don't you tell me about it?"

"I do not know how much I am allowed to say. You see, it involves criminal activity."

"You mean that kidnapping that was on the news? Exciting stuff. She lives on this street, right?"

"Yes. She is a friend."

Cassandra looked around. "This is lovely. Quite unlike other bed and breakfast establishments I've seen. It's clean, crisp, formal, yet still inviting. I'm sure you have a lot to do with the atmosphere, Henrie."

"I do my part."

Annie and Chris returned, Annie carrying a tray with a pitcher, supposedly with top shelf martinis, four glasses, and a shaker with ice. Chris carried a plate of breads and cookies, a few items that remained from the morning.

Annie put the tray in front of Henrie. "Please, Henrie, finish this. You know me. I'll make a mess of it."

"Lemon drop. Quite nice." Henrie poured the liquid into the shaker, shook, and poured glasses. He took his time as he handed one to Cassandra, one to Annie, one to Chris, then served himself. He sat back.

To Henrie's amazement, Annie cut to the chase.

"Cassandra, it's time for you to fess up. What is it that you're after?"

"I beg your pardon?"

"I recognize you from the other night, and several people have let both Henrie and I know that you were asking questions. Mostly about him, but also about me. What do you want?"

Cassandra took a careful sip of her martini. "Quite good, Annie. You're an excellent bartender."

"Not really. Chris pointed out I was about to make a pretty bad gin martini, so I stepped back. Please answer the question. It's late. We've all had a long day."

"So I heard. Well, then, let's get down to it. I'm prepared, Annie, to offer you an outrageous price for this

Inn and everything else that you own. I would like all of your staff to stay on – particularly Henrie – at salaries they have never imagined. I am prepared to offer you a magnificent sum to remain here and manage the properties."

Annie sat back. Both appalled and intrigued.

Then she got a grip on herself and shifted to one hundred percent appalled. She looked at Henrie. "Henrie, are you interested? The higher salary part, especially?"

Henrie looked at Annie steadily for a few seconds. Then he said, "Annie, you are the best owner/manager for whom I have ever worked. You stepped into your father's shoes, and, although I know the two of you worked together to upgrade the facilities, you have taken us to a place none of us could have imagined. We are not at a plateau. We are still growing. I doubt, however, we could grow to a point that increasing pay levels and adding a 'magnificent' salary for you would be sustainable."

"I thought the same. Let's just say for a second that we looked at it and learned that it was sustainable. Would you be interested?"

"No."

Annie looked back at Cassandra. "I'm sorry, Cassandra. The answer is no."

Cassandra sat back, mouth open. For a few seconds, she didn't answer. "I…you…a formal offer has not yet been presented. I'm sure when you see the figures…"

"Let me see," said Annie. I would receive an outrageous sum, and, since I have no significant debt, I would probably become what you call filthy rich. I could continue to live here, I assume, and pay rent, which I assume would be reasonable, and I would receive a magnificent salary to do what I've been doing for a few years. Which is, mostly, to stay out of the way of the people that are trusted to manage the businesses. Is that right, so far?"

"Yes. I think you've got it."

"So I would be a figurehead, working for you, raking it in, and Henrie and the rest of the folks that have done so well for so long will probably be expected to step to a different drummer. The rules would change. Is that on target?"

"Possibly. Well, probably, yes."

"They would be well paid for their efforts. Better paid than what I could manage."

"Yes."

"Then, Cassandra, I suggest, if you are so enamored of the staff, that you offer them your magnificent salaries to go to work for you somewhere else. I don't intend to sell."

"Would you care to think about it for a while?"

Annie and Henrie looked at one another. The lemon drop martini, the stress of the day, and the warmth in his heart for Annie took over.

Henrie looked at Cassandra. "I believe the basic issue, Cassandra, is that neither Annie nor I would work for someone we could not trust. I doubt you will convince any of our current staff to take you up on your offer, either. Although, I expect you would never offer positions unless you owned this particular property. Thank you, but the answer is no."

Henrie and Annie rose and walked out of the room. Chris remained seated. Henrie heard him say, "I'm happy to sit with you until you've finished your drink, Cassandra, then I think we'll say goodnight."

28

Annie, Chris and Henrie hosted an afternoon-into-the-evening bonfire – complete with hot dogs and marshmallows – on the private beach. Almost everyone who lived on or near The Avenue stopped in for a dog and a toasted marshmallow at some point.

It was a celebration of sorts. Halloween was around the corner. The vandalism had come to a stop. Mem was home. She and Frank had nearly healed from their mutual ordeal, and she had sustained no physical injury from Dennis. James was home. Kind of. Unable to get upstairs to their apartment with both legs in casts, he currently stayed in the back downstairs bedroom of the Inn. He faced a long road, but he had a great family and good friends.

There was so much for which to be thankful.

As the afternoon became evening, a handful remained. A small group of friends listened as Jenny told them about her morning meeting.

"I wish you had been there, Annie. It was priceless. I think the entire firm of attorneys turned out for this. WQVX was out for blood."

"You're kidding?"

"Nope. A brace of men in suits on one side of the table and me on the other. They thought they had it in the bag."

"How did you change their minds?"

"Well, first, they had subpoenaed Ian's phone. They took possession last week. I guess, looking at me, they thought they had a rube in the room. When they said you would be sued to the extent of the law, I asked if they had looked at the evidence. They, of course, said there was nothing on the phone to implicate anyone but you, Annie, but, oh my, where did that phone go? Did you bring it, Joe? No, I thought you had it. Then a telephone call to their office, and the evidence is gone! Just like that! Lost!"

"And you said…"

"And I said, no problem. I have the photos right here. I brought out my portable projector and showed them on the wall."

"All of them?"

"Start to finish. And I gave color commentary, first giving the station a plug. I told them I was sure their video prior to the situation would show no confrontation whatsoever. But then I started the slide show. We went in slow motion. I said, look, here Annie is smiling but Dan looks frustrated. And here, Annie leans down to pick up her water bottle, and Dan makes a fist. Here. Right here. And here, Annie starts to come up, and Dan's arm is moving forward. There, he connects, his fist to her head. Watch this…she reels back a little bit…and now she recovers. There. That's her recovery. Water bottle connects to the nose."

The group was laughing now, but Jenny wasn't finished.

"They argued about the timing of everything, that perhaps I had altered the order of the photos. So we looked at each one, full stop, and watched the time stamp change from photo to photo. Did you know they stamp in seconds?"

"Did that finish them?"

"No. They said I didn't have the original photos, and I couldn't go into court with copies. And I said well, you'll have to explain to the court how and why you lost subpoenaed evidence."

"They didn't have a chance."

"No, they didn't. I had affidavits from Ian and George that Ian had downloaded these photos at this time to George's computer, and that George had turned it over to me. And I added an additional affidavit from you, Pete. That you had viewed the photos from his phone and made a copy of them yourself before turning it over to the prosecutor."

"Busted."

"Busted. They're going to talk about settling, Annie."

Annie was stunned. "I'm going to have to pay them?"

"No. They're going to make an offer to pay you, in the hope you won't sue them."

The cats leaned into Cyril and Jock. Their humans were on the private beach having a bonfire.

As Tiger Lily kneaded Cyril's shoulder, she said, *"We were really mad that Mommy went on the boat without us."*

Jock was a tease. He said, *"We had a great time, didn't we, Cyril? The stars, then the full moon, and the lake was so pleasant."*

Little Socks bopped Jock on the nose. She didn't use her claws, though.

Mr. Bean said, *"Mommy said she would find Daryll a fur-ever home. I wish he could stay with us."*

Daryll purred, happy to be curled into Jock's chest.

Cyril, who was always wise, said, *"Your mom can't take all the cats and dogs that show up here. She'd have to get licensed as a kennel, and probably the guests would stop coming."*

"I guess you're right. But still...."

Cyril said, *"Did you hear about Dennis?"*

"No. What now?"

"He's going into a witness protection program."

"Wot's dat?"

"He'll work with some federal people and tell them everything he knows about the men that wanted money. And in return, they'll give him a new identity."

"He'll get a new name?"

"Everything will be different. Name, home. He won't ever be able to contact people he knows again. No one will know where he is."

"And Mem will be safe."

"Supposedly."

Jock thought about something and started to chuckle, deep in his chest.

Tiger Lily asked, *"What's funny?"*

"I just thought about your Mom breaking that guy's nose, and all of you were looking in the other direction. You're great detectives."

Jock's laugh rumbled deeper.

The cats huffed to themselves and decided it might be better to just take a nap. Silence was punctuated by yawns, sighs, sounds of cats cleaning themselves and a purr or two.

Someone came in the front door. Kali and Ko shook themselves awake and trotted to the foyer. It was their job to greet guests, after all.

It wasn't a guest. Not really. Ko greeted Martha while Kali said hello to Speckles. *"Hi, Speckles. We haven't seen you for a while."*

"I've been real busy. It's tough being a single nanny kitty. I need help!"

Martha put Little Fred's carrier on the floor, the better for Kali and Ko to say hello, then left the foyer to look for Henrie.

Kali and Ko were Little Fred's first nanny kitties, when she stayed at the Inn with her mother. When Georgia and Little Fred moved to Martha's house, Kali and Ko trained Speckles for the job.

Kali nosed Little Fred for a while and dropped a paper butterfly into her carrier. She then turned to Speckles. *"You're right. Being a nanny kitty is tough. It took both of us, and sometimes we had to ask for help."*

Ko added sagely, *"Especially when she pooped."*

"Yeah. When she pooped was the worst. One of us had to stay…"

"She had to hold onto a tail when she cried…"

"And one of us would run tell Georgia…"

"Or Henrie…"

"Or Mommy…"

"And sometimes no one would come, and we had to…"

"...*get all the kitty cats to help us yell for help.*"

"*Yeah. I miss those days.*"

Speckles sat down and looked at the two big girls. "*So you know how hard it is for me. I'm just one kitty. She has to hold onto my tail.*"

"*So what do you do?*"

"*I just sit right there and scream until someone hears me.*"

Kali nodded in sympathy. "*It's tough work, that's for sure.*"

Ko, not usually known for her brilliance, sat up with a bright face. "*I know!*" She ran to the library calling for Daryll.

"*What?*" A startled Daryll sat up, bopping Jock in the chin in the process.

"*Come out here! Meet Speckles and Martha! This could be your fur-ever home!*"

Tiger Lily said, "*Smile. Put your best foot forward.*"

Daryll, becoming more confident every day, followed Ko at a trot. He slowed down when he saw Speckles and the thing in the rocking box.

Martha returned to the foyer. She looked down at the little cat and said, "Look at you. Aren't you cute? When did Annie get you?"

Daryll answered politely. "*I'm just staying until I find a fur-ever home.*"

Martha heard "Ick ick meow purr."

"You're so cute. Well, I just stopped in to visit. I couldn't get here in time for a hot dog, but I'll bet they saved me a marshmallow. Will you kids watch Little Fred for a minute?"

Martha made sure Little Fred was secure in the library and promised to be back soon.

Speckles and Daryll looked at one another. They were both young, both small. One girl and one boy. They started to chase each other around the foyer, library and dining room.

Speckles showed off her ninja abilities, jumping, turning in mid-air and diving to swipe Darryl's nose with a right cross.

Daryll busted a move he had previously not shown in the Inn. He lay in wait behind a door, wiggling in anticipation, until Speckles ran in. In one swift movement, he jumped into the air, four legs outstretched, and landed full force on her back.

Kali and Ko sat back, pleased. *"See?"* said Ko. *"They're going to be great friends."*

Annie came in with Martha to take a look at Little Fred. "She's getting so big. How can you even pick her up?"

"I have a rolling cart on the porch. It's a short lift to the platform, and it's real secure. I just push it like a grocery cart."

"Thanks for coming over, Martha. Next time, get here before the hot dogs are gone. Now let's see. Where did Speckles go?"

They looked in the dining room, under the detective table, in the kitchen, went back to the library and out to the all-season porch. No Speckles. Finally, Annie saw two tails on the second floor landing. "She's up there, Martha, and I think she's with our little stray."

They started up the stairs. Martha said, "That cute thing is a stray?"

"Well, kind of. He belonged to the park manager."

"Oh, the one that was…"

"Yeah. Poor little thing needs a new home. He's been here nearly two weeks now. His name is Daryll."

Annie and Martha had reached the landing. Two tails hung down, but the little cats were spooned together, Daryll on the inside and Speckles on the outside.

Annie looked at Martha. "What do you think?"

"I think Daryll has a new home."

29

Chris sat down on the front porch of the Inn. He had chosen the large rocking chair with a matching footrest. He leaned back, closed his eyes, thought about taking a sip of his cold beer, then decided he would prefer to keep his head back and his eyes closed.

Tiger Lily jumped to his lap, apparently to give him something warm to touch.

It was nice to have a normal week on The Avenue. The Inn was full. Everyone seemed nice and boring. They spent time enjoying the lake, local wineries and fall fields.

Chris sighed. He loved Annie, and he loved that she loved her life, but sometimes he could do without the drama. She had been right, though. This time, none of her guests were involved in the criminal activity that was keeping Pete hopping these days.

His cellphone rang. He looked at the display as he answered. "Sam. It's good to hear from you."

Annie's step-father was a good friend. He and Annie's mother came to Chelsea for extended visits several times a year, usually staying in the carriage house.

"Hey, Chris. I wanted to have a quiet word with you. Is Annie around?"

"No, I'm by myself. At the Inn, but on the porch and alone for the moment."

Tiger Lily's claw seemed to come out of nowhere to go into his hand. "Ow! Not quite alone. Tiger Lily is with me."

The claw retracted.

Sam laughed. Then he got down to business. "I wanted to make sure that we aren't going to be an imposition for Thanksgiving."

"Sam, whatever gave you that idea?"

"It's just that, well, you know, we do pay Annie, not as much as her other guests, but we take over the entire place when we all come."

"Trust me, Sam, having the house filled with family is preferable to some of the guests that come. And Annie loves seeing the children."

This was true. Annie loved her nieces and nephews – and her great niece and nephew – even though she needed to take a break from the hubbub every now and then. She was looking forward to hosting the entire family for almost a week.

She was not looking forward as much to the guests that would be in the front room, Chris's parents. Chris didn't think Sam was aware his parents would be there and decided not to share at the moment.

Sam was saying something. "…and Nancy thought she'd bring her new hobby along. She's quilting now."

They talked some more and Sam, having run out of gossip, rang off.

Chris leaned his head back again. He was tired after spending the day decorating The Avenue for the Halloween block party. The Avenue held a charitable party on the last day of every other month. Every year, Halloween seemed to fall on the last day of October. This was a community favorite.

The year before, the Inn had been turned into a haunted house. This year, a walking trail was set up for children of all ages on The Avenue. Businesses on both sides of the street would stay open. Residents and tourists were invited to shop or dine inside or to congregate along the sidewalk or in the median as children walked through to trick-or-treat for UNICEF. Among other things, Chris had been responsible for setting up the kid-friendly zones inside Mo's Tap and Sassy P's.

Now he rested, knowing that he was going to have to get up at some point and put on that ridiculous Zombie outfit and make-up. He and Pete were going to tell ghost stories. Pete would tell stories that involved the town. Chris would tell stories about the haunted shipwrecks of the Great Lakes.

How did he get himself talked into these things?

Ginger and Valeria laughed as they told their stories of the evening. The audience was appreciative. It was a captive audience of one. James.

James was still in the ground level bedroom of the Inn. There were days he appreciated the creature comforts of his new home situation. There were days he grew tired of the constant ministrations of his mother and Annie.

James realized how much he appreciated Henrie. As a teenager, he had often resented the cool, appraising glances, the ability to stay on top of everything, the apparent way he seemed to know everything about everyone. As a young adult and now in need of assistance, James, more than once, was grateful for every time that Henrie showed up – as if by magic – to assist him with…well, let's not go there. Cool and calm was definitely appreciated.

Tonight, James was on the all-season porch, in a back corner, in a comfortable chair with his legs up. He could see and hear what happened on the beach and could watch children and adults as they ran or walked through on their way from the house to the hot dog and marshmallow roast.

Pete and Chris were close enough – in a dark corner just behind the house, and underneath an open window of the porch – that he could hear the ghost stories they spun to groups of all ages.

It never failed. When Pete got to the part about the train robber aiming and shooting, only for the passengers to discover he was a ghost, and when Chris got to the part about the ship rising from the depths, someone screamed.

Now he enjoyed a plate filled with a burger, fries and some kind of pumpkin-on-a-graham-cracker dessert shaped like…a pumpkin.

He looked at his friends. Ginger was dressed as a witch. Long, black dress with jagged edges, purple wig, tall hat, black and orange striped socks and tall clunky shoes. Her broom, child's size, was on the floor at her feet.

Valeria, who had never celebrated Halloween, was stylish in a black turtleneck, black cargo pants, comfortable black tennis shoes and a gold plastic badge affixed to her waist.

Ginger pointed to Valeria's shoes. "See what she's wearing? And now, look at mine." Ginger pointed to clunky platform shoes. "I don't think I'll be able to walk from here to the front door after wearing these all night."

James looked out at the beach. He could see his mother and his two younger siblings as they toasted marshmallows. Carl, his youngest brother, who lived with autism, laughed as his caught on fire.

He turned back to the girls. Ginger was saying, "…the scariest group was inside Mo's. I think they had a lookout that would tell them to get ready."

Valeria continued the story, "So these guys were behind the bar, and as soon as we walked in, one of them jumped up and screamed and the other jumped up behind him with a fake knife and stabbed him."

Ginger took it over, laughing, "And then these two women popped up from the booth on the other side of the kids and screamed like the dickens."

"I had to run after little Sally Morris. She thought someone was really killed in there."

The air in the room changed. James stared in horror as one of his personal nightmares entered the room. Justin.

Ginger and Valeria turned to see what he stared at. They turned in their chairs and scooted closer to James. Ginger, closest to the ghost story window, leaned over and said, "Dad? Dad, can you come in here please?"

From the corner of his eye, James saw two zombies rise as one, look in, and move around the corner to the door.

James stared at Justin, who looked him in the eyes, expression unreadable. When the zombies entered, Justin looked at them. He directed his comments to one of the zombies, who was still, recognizably, the Chief of Police.

"Uh...Chief...I...uh...I came by to pay my respects, and to apologize to James, here, for what happened to him."

Pete nodded. Justin turned back to James.

James heard some of the words. "...sorry...didn't mean...got myself into a bad...anyway...you to know...I'm ready...pay for my crimes...again...sorry you got hurt."

James looked over Justin's shoulder. Henrie stood in the doorway. Silent and steady.

Since a teenager, James knew that without a male role model in his life, he could choose anyone to emulate. Sometimes he chose Pete. Sometimes Ray. Sometimes Chris. Sometimes he chose badly. Tonight, he chose Henrie.

James pulled himself up as straight as he could, with two legs and his left arm in a cast, and looked Justin in the eyes. "I accept your apology, and I am grateful for what you did to end the attack."

Justin nodded. He turned to Ginger. "I need to apologize to you, too, for what I intended to do last year. It was mean, and it could have been hurtful to you for a very long time. I am sincerely sorry for what I put you through."

Ginger looked from Justin to Pete. Just when James thought she would say something hateful, while still looking at Pete she said, "I accept your apology. Don't expect anything else from me."

"I won't. I'm grateful that you accept."

Justin nodded once more to James, then to Pete. He turned and walked off the porch and, presumably, out of the Inn.

Annie was on her hands and knees, reaching underneath a sofa in the foyer. Hilly stopped by on her way out.

"Annie, I'll be here tomorrow. We'll clean up then."

Annie's hand found what she wanted. She grabbed it and pushed herself upright. "I know, Hilly. I just saw this one go under...anyway, I think this is the last one."

Annie opened her hand to show Hilly a bright purple origami butterfly. As she did so, Mr. Bean swooped out of nowhere to grab the butterfly and whisk it to parts unknown.

Annie, at first shocked at the speed of the attack, sat back on her heels to laugh.

Tiger Lily, from the corner, said, *"Mr. Bean, if you keep working on it, you'll be as good a ninja as Speckles."*

Thank You For Reading!

The family of cats and the author hope you enjoyed reading this book as much as we enjoyed writing it!

About The Author

Kathleen Thompson was raised on a small family farm in Indiana. She has an undergraduate degree in Sociology from Manchester College (now Manchester University) and an MBA from Indiana University South Bend.

In a variety of towns and circumstances, she served as a probation officer, parole agent and juvenile residential counselor before moving into administrative, marketing and fund raising positions in human service organizations. Ms. Thompson took a break from human services for seven years to own and operate a bar and restaurant. Let's be honest; that's another type of human service.

While making plans to return to her rural roots, Kathi and her mother discovered an injured kitten at the family farm. The kitten, whose face was a mass of injuries, decided to make Kathi her guardian. She wrapped herself around an ankle, purred like a V8 engine, and wouldn't let go.

Against the advice of her mother, Kathi took the kitten home and to a veterinarian. The vet diagnosed road burn serious enough to take all the fur from the left side of her face, and the kitten – Tiger Lily – eventually healed and took a huge piece of Kathi's heart.

Tiger Lily was joined by the rest, rescue kitties, all: Little Socks (thank you, Aunt Mary); Kali, Ko and Mo (thank you, Connie); Sassy Pants (thank you, Ant Sherwy); and Mr. Bean (thank you, Pulaski Animal Center). Recent arrivals Speckles (thank you, Tennille) and Moriah (thank you again, Pulaski Animal Center) have joined the cast but will not live at the Inn.

Tiger Lily's Café rattled around in Kathi's brain – there isn't much else up there – for all of the years since, sometimes as an actual café and sometimes as a book. It was less expensive to write the book.

Connect with Kathi and her family of cats at their website: www.tigerlilyscafe.com, or find them on Facebook: www.facebook.com/tigerlilyscafemysteries.

Find us on the web: www.tigerlilyscafe.com

Find us on Facebook: Tiger Lily's Café, A Mystery Series by Kathleen Thompson

Text to join: Emails are sent every two weeks. You can opt out at any time. LILYSCAFE to 22828 (You may also sign up for the emails from the website.)

www.ingramcontent.com/pod-product-compliance
Lightning Source LLC
Chambersburg PA
CBHW072204170626
46813CB00003B/780